little
Manhattan
the movie novel

REGENCY ENTERPRISES PRESENTS A PARIAH/NEW REGENCY PRODUCTION
"LITTLE MANHATTAN" JOSH HUTCHERSON BRADLEY WHITFORD CYNTHIA NIXON
MUSIC SUPERVISOR PATRICK HOULIHAN MUSIC BY CHAD FISCHER FILM EDITOR ALAN EDWARD BELL PRODUCTION DESIGNER STUART WURTZEL
DIRECTOR OF PHOTOGRAPHY TIM ORR EXECUTIVE PRODUCERS EZRA SWERDLOW VIVIAN CANNON PRODUCED BY GAVIN POLONE ARNON MILCHAN
PG PARENTAL GUIDANCE SUGGESTED SOME MATERIAL MAY NOT BE SUITABLE FOR CHILDREN Mild Thematic Elements, Language, and Brief Action WRITTEN BY JENNIFER FLACKETT DIRECTED BY MARK LEVIN

www.littlemanhattanmovie.com

Little Manhattan: The Movie Novel

For information address HarperCollins Children's Books, a division of HarperCollins Publishers, 1350 Avenue of the Americas, New York, NY 10019.
Library of Congress catalog card number: 2005924687
www.harperchildrens.com
1 2 3 4 5 6 7 8 9 10
❖
First Edition

little Manhattan

the movie novel

By Judy Katschke

Based on the motion picture written by

Jennifer Flackett

HarperKidsEntertainment

An Imprint of HarperCollins*Publishers*

Gabe was having a bummer of a day.

He couldn't sleep. He couldn't eat. And just a few minutes ago, he was barfing his brains out. And all because he was suffering from a highly contagious disease spread only by girls. It wasn't cooties. Gabe and his friends had survived that epidemic three years ago in the second grade.

Ten-year-old Gabriel Burton was lovesick. And as far as he was concerned—there was no cure!

But things weren't always so glum for Gabe. Only two weeks ago he was a happy-go-lucky kid growing up in New York City, the greatest city in the world.

On the Upper West Side of Manhattan, Gabe had everything a kid could want. With Riverside Park a few blocks west and Central Park a few blocks east, who needed a back and front yard? With half a dozen stores and pizza parlors on every block, who needed a mall? And with a shiny silver scooter that took Gabe anywhere he wanted to go (as long as it was within a nine-block radius), who needed a bike?

To Gabe and his best buds, Max, Sam, and Jacob, the Upper West Side was their oyster. They shot hoops in the schoolyard of P.S. 87, played their trumpets and saxophones in the school jazz ensemble and combed street vendors' tables for vintage comic books. But most of the time they just rode up and down the city streets on their scooters.

"Hey! Hey!" a dog walker shouted. "Watch where you're going!"

Gabe and his crew skillfully veered their scooters around the eight barking dogs. Riding a scooter down a busy street like Broadway was not for wusses!

"You guys!" Max called from his scooter. "Who wants to go to the discount store?"

"Nuh-uh!" Sam shouted over his shoulder. "No way are we helping you steal more chocolate bars!"

"And I'm not doing lookout," Jacob said, firmly.

"Come on, you guys!" Max urged. "You all have no trouble eating the candy I provide for you, right, Gabe?"

But Gabe wasn't thinking about candy. He was

busy checking out the clock on the subway station kiosk. It was already five o'clock and he had somewhere to go. He stuck out his right foot and skidded to a stop.

"I've got to roll, guys," Gabe said.

His friends stopped their scooters one by one. Sam wrinkled his nose in disappointment.

"Where are you going?" Sam asked. "I thought we were going to shoot some twenty-one."

Gabe shook his head. Playing basketball was always cool, but he had other plans. He was going to kick footballs with his dad in Riverside Park.

"I have to meet my dad for practice," Gabe said.

"Practice?" Max laughed out loud. "The two of you are so nuts, man!"

Whatever, Gabe thought as he rode his scooter away.

He knew his friends didn't get it. To them, kicking footballs was no big deal. But to Gabe and his dad, Adam, kicking footballs was all part of a much bigger plan. In ten years Gabe was going to be the Tiger Woods of the place-kicking world.

At first glance Gabe wasn't exactly NFL material. But according to his dad you didn't have to be built like a linebacker to be a good kicker.

"When you've got a good strong leg," his dad would say, "nothing else matters!"

Gabe liked hanging in the park with his dad. With his parents in the process of a divorce, their two-bedroom apartment didn't make for the greatest living environment. Gabe's dad slept on the sofa bed in the living room like some out-of-town guest. His mother had just started dating some jerk named Ronny. To make things even worse, they had separate food in the refrigerator!

At first Gabe didn't get it. How could two people who had fallen madly in love at summer camp more than twenty years ago grow to despise each other so much? But one day while watching his parents fight over the *New York Times* crossword puzzle, Gabe reached a profound conclusion:

Love ends. Period.

In the meantime, Gabe and his parents had worked out a pretty good system. Tuesdays, Thursdays, and Saturdays were for him and his mom. Mondays, Wednesdays, and Fridays were for him and his dad. And Sundays were exclusively for Gabe.

"Hey, Dad!" Gabe called as he rolled his scooter into the park. Adam was already in their usual place, sticking a plastic tee into the ground. He reached into his bag of pigskins for a football as Gabe ran over.

"Hey, champ!" Adam said with a grin. "Ready?"

"Ready!" Gabe replied, dropping his scooter on the grass.

Adam got down on one knee. He steadied the football on the tee and waited until Gabe gave it a hard, swift boot.

Gabe smiled as the ball sailed across the field and between the orange pylons.

"Sweet!" Gabe exclaimed.

Adam reached into his sack for another ball. "If you dedicate yourself to one goal and only one goal from an early age," he said, "you can achieve anything, champ."

The sun glowed red as it sank over the New Jersey Palisades and the Hudson River. But Gabe and his dad kept on practicing.

"Gabriel Burton from twenty-three yards to win the game!" Gabe shouted behind the football. "Can he do it, ladies and gentlemen?"

Gabe gritted his teeth as he booted a twenty-yarder between the pylons. He threw up his arms in victory. Adam lifted him on his shoulder to celebrate.

"You're the man!" Adam cheered.

After some more impressive kicks and goals, it was

time to head home. Adam collected the footballs and stuffed them back into the bag. Gabe hopped back on his scooter. Then they left the field and Riverside Park.

"How did it get so late?" Adam asked as they strolled past the stoops of old brownstones. "Your mom's probably got dinner waiting for you. Hey, I have an idea. Why don't we stop for a slice of pizza on the way?"

Gabe took a deep breath as he rolled his scooter on the sidewalk. It was time to ask his dad a question he had meant to ask him days ago. . . .

"Dad?" Gabe asked slowly. "Can I take . . . karate?"

Adam stopped walking. He stared down at Gabe.

"Karate?" he asked. "What does karate have to do with place kicking?"

Gabe shrugged. He knew karate had nothing to do with football. But it had a lot to do with the bane of his existence, Daryl Kitzens!

Daryl was the scariest kid on the Upper West Side—possibly in all of Manhattan. He had been in the fifth grade but was left back so many times that he should have been in the seventh! Daryl was an evil giant who lived to torture others—especially when it came to dodgeball.

Gabe shuddered as he remembered being pummeled by Daryl's hurling ball.

"I don't know, Dad," Gabe said. "But it can't hurt."

Gabe watched his dad from the corner of his eye as they kept on walking. Adam seemed to be thinking about it.

After a minute that seemed more like an hour, Adam finally asked, "How much does it cost?"

Gabe grinned. When his dad asked that question, it usually meant one thing. *Yes!*

"Does that mean I can?" Gabe asked.

"Not if I'm going to pay an arm and a leg," Adam said. "But if it's reasonable . . ."

"Thanks, Dad!" Gabe said.

Gabe and his dad reached their building on West End Avenue. They walked into the lobby and greeted Ralph, the elevator operator. Ralph chatted as he piloted the elevator straight up to the eighth floor. Adam used his keys to unlock the door to their apartment. As they entered Gabe saw his mom in the kitchen. She was home from her job as a physical therapist.

Leslie stopped cutting mushrooms to kiss Gabe. Adam did what he usually did when he came home from practice—he tossed his bag of footballs into the closet, and then combed through the refrigerator.

"Hey, Leslie!" Adam shouted, his head inside the fridge. "You drank my Pepsi!"

Uh-oh, Gabe thought. *Here we go.*

"Excuse me," Leslie said. She planted her hands on her hips. "But it was my Pepsi."

"It had my name on it!" Adam argued back.

Gabe rolled his eyes to the ceiling. It got to the point where his mom and dad were actually labeling their food. Now they were fighting over a missing Pepsi bottle!

Pathetic!

Gabe couldn't wait to start his karate class now.

It would not only be fun and practical, it would be another way to escape his dysfunctional family life.

Little did he know that his karate class would be the biggest mistake he ever made!

2

Gabe sat cross-legged on the floor of the karate studio. He thought the day would never come. But here it was—his first karate class!

He checked out the other kids sitting around him. They were all about his age and wore white belts just like him.

Gabe knew his white belt was only temporary. In a few days he'd be a yellow belt. Then, a brown belt. And eventually a black belt!

In your face, Daryl Kitzens! Gabe thought.

Everyone stopped talking when the instructor, Master Coles, stepped to the front of the studio. Gabe and the other kids couldn't take their eyes off of his black belt.

"Karate is not about strength," Master Coles

began. "It's about skill. It's about focus. It's an art of determination."

The door swung open. A girl with long dark hair hurried into the studio. Gabe recognized her right away. It was Rosemary Telesco from his class at school. Right behind her was her nanny, Birdie, and her little sister, Mae-Li. The Telescos had adopted Mae-Li in China when she was just a baby.

"Sorry, Master Coles," Rosemary said. "My tap class was late."

Master Coles and Rosemary nodded to each other. Then, Rosemary walked to an empty space in the back of the class.

Gabe smiled. It was good to see a familiar face, especially on his first day of class, when the only kid he knew was his own reflection in the mirror. But, as the hour went by, Gabe felt more and more comfortable in the karate studio on the floor above the stereo store.

Master Coles demonstrated the basic karate stances and moves. As the kids practiced them, he spoke about the discipline of karate. And about the belts!

"Those of you who pass the test to get your yellow

belt will get yellow," Master Coles said. "Those who pass red will get red. It's about finding your personal best."

As Gabe practiced his hand moves in front of the mirror, he was at peace with the world—until Master Coles demonstrated sparring techniques and announced, "I want you all to pair up. Everyone gets a sparring partner."

Pair up? Gabe gulped.

He watched the other kids quickly coupling up around him. Without a partner he felt like a total loser.

That's when he saw Rosemary Telesco standing alone in the studio.

"Hey," Gabe mumbled.

"Hey," Rosemary said.

I don't want a girl for a sparring partner! Gabe thought. *What guy would?* But with no guys left, Gabe didn't have much of a choice. The two stepped up to each other. Before Gabe could take a stance, Rosemary grabbed hold of him and flipped him to the mat!

WHAM!

Rosemary repeated the move a half-dozen times. As Gabe's head slammed against the mat, his life with

Rosemary Telesco flashed before his eyes. And Rosemary was in his life for as long as he could remember.

First, there was nursery school. Gabe and Rosemary had their share of play dates. One date resulted in a colorful finger painting on the Burton dining room wall.

Next, there was kindergarten. Then the first grade. Then second grade. All the way up to fifth. Rosemary was in Gabe's class every single year, and Gabe had the class pictures to prove it.

But as the years went by, Gabe had hardly noticed Rosemary. Not that she wasn't pretty. She just wasn't the prettiest girl in the class. The prettiest girl was Madison Shaw, with her long blond hair and sparkling green eyes. The second prettiest was Vanessa Muir with her glossy black hair and jet brown eyes.

Rosemary was more like the third prettiest girl in the class. Gabe figured if there were medals for cuteness, she would probably win the bronze.

But, boy, Gabe thought as he stood up from the mat, *can that girl do karate!*

"Keep your elbow tucked, Gabe," Master Coles said as Gabe and Rosemary circled each other. "Very nice, Rosemary. Your fist should be a hammer . . . tighter."

For the next few classes, Gabe and Rosemary stayed sparring partners. They kicked together, thrusted together, and chopped together. There was just one little problem.

When it came to karate, Rosemary was as awesome as a ninja street fighter.

"Yaaa!" Rosemary yelled, as she smashed through a wooden plank with her hand.

And Gabe was . . . awful.

"Yow!" Gabe cried, as he smashed his hand right into the plank.

Gabe's buddies knew about Rosemary, but he didn't want them to get the wrong idea. He and Rosemary weren't really friends. They were just karate friends.

So as Gabe shot hoops with his friends in the schoolyard, Rosemary hung out with her friends on the swings. The two hardly glanced at each other or even said hi. But after school, when they put on their white robes and belts, they could see past their many differences and fight as equals.

Well, almost equals . . .

"We all congratulate Rosemary on being the first in class to earn her yellow belt," Master Coles said. *"Kanakawa!"*

"*Kanakawa!*" the kids repeated.

Rosemary beamed as Master Coles handed her a yellow belt. Everyone watched as she tied it around her waist.

Gabe sighed as he gazed down at his white belt. Sure, he was happy for Rosemary. But if this didn't make him feel like a total loser, he didn't know what did!

After class Gabe and Rosemary left the studio together. Gabe rolled his scooter on the sidewalk as he walked alongside Rosemary. Trailing behind them were Birdie and Rosemary's little sister, Mae-Li.

"Girls mature faster than boys, you know," Rosemary said matter-of-factly.

Gabe laughed out loud. "Is that a fact?" he asked.

"Actually," Rosemary said, "I think it is."

Gabe groaned under his breath. What was she talking about? Was the yellow belt going straight to her head?

"That is completely made up," Gabe argued. "Boys are so much more mature than girls."

Rosemary turned to Gabe and shook her head. "This isn't a matter of opinion, Gabe," she said. "There were studies done. Girls speak before boys do. They walk before boys do, too."

"And how do you know?" Gabe asked.

Rosemary nodded over her shoulder at her little sister. "I see it in my sister's preschool class all the time," she said. "The boys her age all seem . . . almost backward."

Gabe squeezed the handlebar of his scooter. *Okay*, he thought angrily, *now it's getting personal!*

"You are such a loser!" Gabe declared.

"Truth hurts, my friend," Rosemary said.

Gabe stuck his chin out and said, "There is absolutely no reason I shouldn't be able to get my yellow belt in a week."

"No way," Rosemary scoffed. "You don't take karate seriously enough."

"Take it seriously?" Gabe cried.

"You're not focused," Rosemary explained calmly. "You don't practice."

"I practice," Gabe said.

"When?" Rosemary asked.

"All the time," Gabe said.

"You should practice with me," Rosemary said. "You'd get much better, you know."

Wait a minute, Gabe thought. *Who does she think she is?*

But Gabe was sick of all the verbal sparring. He

heard enough of that at home!

Who knows? Gabe thought. *Maybe practicing with Rosemary isn't such a bad idea. She is good. And she is the first yellow belt in the class.*

"Fine," Gabe blurted out. "Let's practice."

"Name the time," Rosemary said.

"I don't care," Gabe said. "Now?"

"Fine," Rosemary said.

"Great," Gabe said.

He and Rosemary were quiet as they continued walking up Broadway. Suddenly Rosemary said, "Oh, I forgot! I have to do this errand."

"What kind of errand?" Gabe asked.

"I'm supposed to be a flower girl in a couple of weeks," Rosemary said. She didn't look too thrilled. "I'm being fitted for this dress."

"Oh," Gabe said.

"It'll only take about five minutes," Rosemary said. "I promise."

Classic female move. *The bait and switch*, Gabe thought. *Mom conned me into many a shoe store with that one!*

It was always the shoe store first, then ice cream. But was there anything worse than dress shopping?

Gabe trembled as he followed Rosemary and her nanny to the bridal shop. Before going inside he glanced over both shoulders. If Max, Sam, or Jacob saw him going into a girls' dress store with a girl, he'd be toast!

The coast was clear. Gabe slipped into the store. While Rosemary talked to a salesgirl, he plopped himself into a pink-and-gold, satiny chair. To Gabe, there was nothing worse than dress shopping. In fact, he would much rather have his toenails peeled off one by one with pliers than spend five minutes in a dress store!

"Give me a break," Gabe muttered to himself.

Birdie sat in the next chair working on her needlepoint. Mae-Li was running in and out of the dress racks, laughing as clouds of chiffon tickled her face.

Is this some kind of nightmare? Gabe wondered. *What am I doing here? Help me!*

A red velvet curtain in the back of the store parted. Gabe's mouth dropped open as Rosemary stepped out. She was wearing a long purple dress and looked amazing.

"Pretty!" Mai-Li squealed.

That's for sure! Gabe thought.

He couldn't stop staring at Rosemary as she twirled in front of a full-length mirror.

"So," Rosemary asked Gabe, "what do you think?"

Gabe opened his mouth to speak.

Nothing came out.

But being speechless wasn't Gabe's only problem . . .

What is this feeling in my stomach? Gabe wondered. *This . . . this lightening bolt? Who is this creature before me?*

③

"**U**m . . . um . . . ," Gabe stammered.

His mouth felt as dry as cotton. He could feel beads of sweat forming on his forehead and his upper lip.

"Oh, Rosemary!" Birdie exclaimed. She laid her needlepoint in her lap and clasped her hands together. "You are going to be the prettiest flower girl at the wedding!"

"Definitely the oldest one," Rosemary said sarcastically.

Gabe knew he had to say something. Anything!

"Um," Gabe said. "Wh-who's getting married?"

"My mom's sister," Rosemary replied. "She's been engaged for years. . . ."

Rosemary's mouth was moving, but Gabe heard

nothing. He was too busy thinking how pretty she looked. Prettier than Vanessa Muir. Even prettier than Madison Shaw. In just a matter of minutes, Rosemary Telesco had leaped to first place!

Rosemary used her parents' credit card to pay for the dress. Birdie carried the shopping bag as they all left the bridal shop.

Gabe was still tongue-tied as he rode his scooter alongside Rosemary.

She's a girl, Gabe thought. *I'm supposed to hate girls. Not feel nervous talking to one!*

He looked sideways at Rosemary. She was back to wearing her street clothes, but to Gabe she still looked like that awesome girl in the purple dress.

This is Rosemary Telesco! Gabe thought. *I've known her since nursery school. Practically my whole life!*

Suddenly Gabe felt the scooter slip out from under his feet. He gnashed his teeth as he hit the pavement with a loud thud.

"Gabe!" Rosemary cried.

Birdie and Mai-Li ran over.

"Are you okay?" Birdie asked.

Gabe forced a smile as he leaped up to his feet. Falling off your scooter was bad enough. Falling off your scooter in front of a pretty girl, her nanny, and her little sister was a fate worse than death.

"Hey, I'm cool!" Gabe said with a chuckle. "Just a scrape."

Gabe decided to walk his scooter the rest of the way to Rosemary's building. The Telescos lived in a fancy building on Central Park West and West 81st Street, right across the street from the planetarium. Mr. and Mrs. Telesco were the executive producers of the hottest daytime soap opera on TV. They didn't send Rosemary to private school. Instead they sent her to P.S. 87 because they believed in public education. Gabe's family didn't have a choice.

A white-gloved doorman tapped the brim of his hat as the four of them entered the building. Gabe held his breath as he rode up in the elegant elevator. It wasn't the creaky metal cage like the one in Gabe's building. And it didn't have a chatty elevator guy named Ralph either. Instead it had wood paneling, soft lighting—and music. It was just elevator music, but who cared when you were riding up in style?

Birdie opened the door to the Telesco apartment. Gabe followed Rosemary inside. From where he stood he could see a big picture window overlooking Central Park. And as Rosemary walked him through the richly carpeted rooms, it became pretty clear. The

Telescos had big bucks!

"Let's go to my room," Rosemary suggested. "So we can start practicing."

Rosemary's room was a study in pink. Pink shag rug, pink bedspread, pink curtains.

Gabe tried to focus on karate as he and Rosemary sparred. As Master Coles said, karate was all about focus. But all Gabe could focus on was Rosemary.

Bam, bam, bam!

Gabe hit the shag rug over and over. But he didn't care. His head was filled with thoughts of Rosemary.

He wanted to know, *Who is she? Why does she have this strange power over me? What is that smell? Is it strawberry? Is it her smell?*

Bam, bam, bam!

When practice was over, Gabe went to the bathroom. While he was in there, he decided to search for clues that would solve the mystery of Rosemary.

The medicine cabinet squeaked slightly as Gabe opened it. Luckily there was nothing too embarrassing inside. Just the usual boring drugstore stuff—ace bandages, cold pills, ointments . . . and a tiny pot of pink lip gloss, just like the color of Rosemary's room.

He unscrewed the lid and took a whiff. Strawberry. It smelled just like Rosemary.

Gabe closed his eyes as he inhaled the sweet scent dreamily. His eyes popped open when he heard a noise outside the door. He quickly screwed the lid back on and shoved the pot of gloss back in the cabinet.

"Hey," Gabe said, as he joined Rosemary in her stainless-steel state-of-the-art kitchen. Rosemary was seated at the counter eating cookies and drinking milk. Birdie and Mae-Li were sculpting with Play-Doh at the table.

Gabe climbed up onto a high stool next to Rosemary. He helped himself to a cookie.

"So," Rosemary said after a gulp of milk, "what made you take karate?"

"Daryl Kitzens," Gabe said through a mouth full of cookie crumbs.

Rosemary laughed. "Daryl Kitzens made you take karate?" she asked. "No way!"

The thought of Daryl attacking him in dodgeball made Gabe's legs ache. "Have you seen the guy?" he cried. "He's a madman! Insane!"

Rosemary's eyes twinkled as she said, "Afraid he's going to beat you up?"

Great, Gabe thought. *Now she thinks I'm a wuss!*

"Of course not!" Gabe blurted. "I'm not afraid of

him at all. I just want to be ready when the day comes."

Gabe coolly dunked a second cookie into his glass of milk.

Who am I kidding? he thought. *I'm terrified of the guy!*

When they finished the plate of cookies, Rosemary hopped off her stool. "So . . . um," she said. "Should we practice again?"

Gabe's eyebrows flew up. There was nothing he wanted to do more than practice karate with Rosemary again. Even if it meant getting his head slammed into her floor over and over again. But he couldn't seem too psyched. That wouldn't be cool.

"Whatever, y'know," Gabe said. "If you want."

Rosemary glanced at the clock on the wall. "Actually," she said, "it's getting kind of late."

Gabe's heart sank.

"Late, yeah," he said, climbing off his chair. "I've got to be going, too. Okay. Right, yeah."

As they walked through the kitchen Gabe kept his eyes on the back of Rosemary's head. Her hair was so shiny. So thick. So—

"Ow!" Gabe cried as he bumped into a glass wall.

Rosemary whirled around.

"Oh," Gabe said, feeling like a jerk. "That's the . . . um . . . wall."

Rosemary giggled. Then she waved Gabe out of the kitchen. As they walked through the apartment Gabe checked out the family pictures on the walls: Rosemary's parents in black tie, holding Daytime Emmy awards. Birdie holding a baby Rosemary. The Telescos in front of the Great Wall of China with their new baby, Mae-Li.

Look at her, Gabe thought. *Living this perfect life up here. With her view of the park and everything. Yet she's so down-to-earth.*

Suddenly, Rosemary's whole world seemed very attractive to Gabe.

Her parents with all their success! Gabe thought. *The nanny who's been with her since she was born. The adopted three-year-old sister rescued from an orphanage in Beijing!*

Gabe walked past the pictures and sighed. *And me*, he thought glumly. *My family's on a one-way ticket to the Jerry Springer Show!*

"See you," Rosemary said at the door.

"See you," Gabe said, grabbing his scooter.

As Gabe left the building on West 81st Street, a goofy grin spread across his face. Scooting back to his building, everything looked the same—the streets, the people, even the stores. But something that afternoon was very different. And that something was Gabe. He was in love for the first time in his whole life.

And so far it felt pretty good!

4

As great as Gabe felt, he still didn't get it. How did this happen to him? How could he be in love?

But Gabe didn't dwell on the question for too long. Instead he spent his time daydreaming about Rosemary. And "casually" riding his scooter past her building practically every day now that it was finally summer and there was no school.

Rosemary lived on West 81st Street, justt north of the planetarium. That was just a few yards north of the area his parents allowed him to roam within.

Gabe's territory ended with the planetarium to the north, Riverside Park to the west, Central Park to the east, and 67th Street to the south. Gabe never really minded the restrictions. There were plenty of cool things to do within his permitted radius. And now there was one more cool thing he could do: stake out Rosemary's building from across the street!

By now Gabe knew just about every crack in the sidewalk as he kicked his scooter northward toward West 81st Street. On those blocks he felt like he owned the town.

But it wasn't always that way. When Gabe first started riding to Rosemary's building he felt like he was heading into uncharted waters. He would hide across the street behind a thick tree trunk. Peeking out, he would always see the doormen, standing at attention under the green awning like white-gloved soldiers guarding a fort.

I don't know what I'm hoping for, Gabe thought, slumping against the tree. *A glimpse of Rosemary? A chance encounter?*

Gabe wasn't sure. But with each day he felt more and more desperate!

School is over. *It's summer break*, Gabe thought, lurking in the shadow of the tree. *Our next karate class isn't for three days. Three days—that's forever!*

Drastic situations called for drastic measures. So after another day of no Rosemary sightings, Gabe scooted home and called every Telesco in the phone book. All two of them!

One Mr. Telesco was a butcher down in Greenwich Village. Gabe could practically smell the bloody meat in the store as he answered the phone. Another Mr. Telesco was an elderly guy who wasn't too happy to hear from Gabe. . . .

"Um . . . er . . . is R-Rosemary there?" Gabe stammered.

"Hey! You the kid who called half an hour ago?" Mr. Telesco demanded. "You little—"

Gabe slammed down the receiver. He was out of Telescos but he wouldn't give up. Rosemary had to be out there somewhere!

So next he dialed the operator.

"Listing, please," the operator said.

"The name is Telesco," Gabe explained. "West Eighty-first Street. Or maybe it's Central Park West."

Gabe bit his nails as the operator searched her database. Rosemary's number had to be listed somewhere!

"Here's the number," the operator finally said. "Yes, West Eighty-first Street."

"You found it?" Gabe squeaked. He wanted to jump up and shout for joy, as if he had just won the New York Lottery. Until—

"I'm sorry," the operator said. "That number is unlisted."

Gabe sighed heavily as he hung up the phone. Rosemary Telesco was so close . . . yet so far!

For the next three days Gabe didn't feel like hanging out with Max. Or Sam. Or Jacob. All he felt like doing was thinking about Rosemary.

One hot day Gabe was gliding his scooter in lazy circles on Central Park West. He glanced up at Rosemary's building and balked. The doorman was looking straight at him!

He was about to turn his scooter around when he saw three people emerge from the building. It was Birdie, Mae-Li, and Rosemary!

Omigosh! Gabe thought. *There she is!*

Gabe froze on his scooter like a deer in headlights. Should he turn and ride away? Or stick around and act coolly surprised to see Rosemary?

Gabe didn't know what to do. He didn't have a plan ready in case he actually saw Rosemary.

Just go up to her, Gabe thought, his heart pounding under his T-shirt. *Go. Go. And say hi.*

Instead, Gabe gave a kick and scooted away.

Coward! Fool! How can you be so weak? Gabe shouted inside his head. *I'm not weak—I'm human. What was I going to say? I was in the neighborhood? That's so pathetic!*

Gabe kicked harder and harder as he argued with himself.

No! I'm weak and pathetic and I'm going to be alone my entire life! Who cares if I'm alone? I'd rather be alone than endure this misery and torment—

He swerved around a corner and his jaw dropped. Coming down the block was Birdie, Mae-Li, and Rosemary!

"Whoa!" Gabe cried.

Birdie grabbed Mae-Li's hand as the three jumped aside.

"Gabe?" Rosemary asked.

Gabe fought to regain his balance. "How's it going?" he asked. "Hi . . . I was just . . . you know, in the neighborhood."

Rosemary wrinkled her nose. "Don't you live in the neighborhood?" she asked.

Gabe forced a smile, but what he really wanted to do was curl up and die!

"Oh, sure," Gabe said. "Seventy-third and West End. Guess it depends on how, um, neighborhood is defined. . . ."

Birdie raised an eyebrow.

Great, Gabe thought. *Now her nanny thinks I'm nuts!*

"So . . . what are you up to?" Gabe asked.

Rosemary nodded at Mae-Li. "My sister's got a birthday party in Central Park," she said in a blasé voice. "Want to come?"

"Come . . . to the party?" Gabe asked. If there was anything worse than medieval torture, it was a party full of screaming preschoolers. But with Rosemary there, he could deal with anything!

"I'm there," Gabe said with a smile.

They headed one block east to Central Park. Mae-Li's party was already set up under a big shady tree tied with balloons. Under the tree were two long tables. One was covered with cake, cookies, and punch. Another one was covered with brightly wrapped presents for the birthday girl.

Gabe and Rosemary sat on the grass. They watched the kids as they hopped up and down around the Bubble Lady, a woman blowing bubbles into amazing shapes.

"Look," Rosemary said. She nodded toward the kids. "There's an example of my point about girls maturing faster than boys. Those two kids are the same age. The little girl is talking up a storm, and the little boy is just drooling over his cupcake."

Here we go, Gabe thought. *The maturity issue!*

"They're not the same age," Gabe said, shaking his head.

Rosemary turned to face Gabe. "Oh, yeah?" she asked. "How much do you want to bet?"

Gabe looked at Rosemary, and then at the little kids they were talking about. "A buck says he's six months younger," he said.

"Buy me an ice cream?" Rosemary said.

"Nuh-uh!" Gabe said. "You're buying me one!"

Rosemary and Gabe walked over to a bunch of mothers sitting on a picnic blanket.

"Excuse me," Rosemary said to one of the moms. "Is that your little boy over there? How old is he?"

The woman took off her sunglasses and smiled. "He's two and a half," she said.

Rosemary then pointed to the girl, who was chasing a floating bubble. "And do you know how old that little girl is?" she asked.

"Oh, she's about three months younger than he is," the mom said. "Ethan's birthday is in September. Gracie's birthday is in December."

As they walked away from the blanket, Rosemary whispered, "You owe me!"

"That proves nothing," Gabe said.

Rosemary didn't say a word. She just smiled as she

watched the little kids frolicking on the grass.

Gabe smiled, too—as he watched Rosemary.

Look at her, Gabe thought. *I have never seen anyone more beautiful. She's just my type too!*

Hey, wait a minute. Gabe didn't even know he had a type.

His thoughts turned to other pretty girls. Betty in the *Archie* comics. Jan Brady. Mary Ann from *Gilligan's Island*. All brainy and beautiful.

He studied Rosemary; the was sun glinting off her long, dark hair. She wasn't overwhelmingly beautiful. Just "enough" beautiful. And that was enough for him.

Gabe glanced over at Birdie sitting near them and knitting.

Now if I could just shake the nanny, we'd be in business, Gabe thought.

"Rosemary?" Gabe piped up. "Do you think we should get some ice cream?"

"Now?" Rosemary asked.

"Sure," Gabe said with a small shrug. "A bet's a bet, right?"

Rosemary turned to Birdie. "Birdie, can we get ice cream?" she called.

Birdie looked at the ice cream stand up the path. She reached into her pocket and pulled out a five-dollar bill.

"You come right back now," Birdie said.

"Thanks," Gabe said, waving away the money. "Unfortunately, this one's on me."

As the two walked toward the ice cream stand, Gabe reached into his pocket for a crisp five-dollar bill. There would be no watery ice pops for them. Or bright yellow popsicles that looked like goofy smiley faces. It would be Häagen Dazs dark chocolate bars all the way!

This is a special occasion, Gabe thought. *It's my first date!*

Gabe bought chocolate ice cream bars for Rosemary and himself. That was the easy part.

So how come I have nothing to say to her? Gabe wondered, as he and Rosemary ate their ice cream. *Why am I just talking to myself? Why aren't I talking to her? Why isn't she looking at me? Am I that hideous? Do I smell?*

Gabe swallowed hard. This wasn't as easy as he thought it would be, the way dates always seem on TV and in the movies. He and Rosemary had known each other forever and yet had nothing to talk about.

Rosemary finally glanced at Gabe. It was an uncomfortable glance—as if she was thinking the same thing.

I have to say something once and for all, Gabe thought. *Anything!*

"So," Gabe said, "you come here often?"

"Central Park?" Rosemary asked, surprised.

Gabe wanted to smack himself in the head. What kind of a lame question was that? Every kid on the Upper West Side practically grew up in Central Park. He did. Rosemary did. How could he be such a cheese head?

"Um . . . yeah," Gabe said.

"I do live across the street, you know," Rosemary said. "How about you?"

"Me?" Gabe asked.

"Do you go to Riverside Park?" Rosemary asked.

"Yeah," Gabe said. "I'm a Riverside guy. But Central Park is pretty cool, too. I've done my time here."

Gabe felt himself loosening up. He wasn't exactly an expert on girls yet, but he did consider himself an expert on Central Park.

"Strawberry Fields," Gabe pointed out. "What was it named for?"

"Some Beatles song, right?" Rosemary asked.

"It was actually named after this orphanage in

Liverpool," Gabe explained, "where John Lennon used to play with his friends, who lived there."

Rosemary's face brightened. "Really?" she asked. "I've passed it a million times and never knew that."

Gabe smiled as he crunched into his ice cream bar. About a year and half ago he read two books about the island of Manhattan. He also wrote a book report on the subject, which definitely made him a man in his element!

Gabe and Rosemary strolled side by side through Strawberry Fields. They circled the mosaic plaque in the concrete ground. The word in the middle read "Imagine." Colorful flowers had been strewn on the plaque, and people were sitting around it playing guitars and singing Beatles songs.

Gabe and Rosemary listened to the music as they finished their ice cream. They tossed the wrappers into a trash can and began walking up the path. It led them to a rolling green lawn called Sheep Meadow.

"Did you know that there used to be real sheep grazing here?" Gabe asked. He pointed to a brick house, which was now a restaurant. "And the herder used to live up there."

"Real sheep in Central Park?" Rosemary asked. Her dark eyes lit up. "No way!"

"Way," Gabe said, nodding. "The herder was eventually given a job in the lion house at the zoo."

Rosemary giggled as they walked on. Gabe could practically see the fluffy white sheep on the green lawn. As they walked under a footbridge, Gabe felt great. He was taking Rosemary on a grand tour of Central Park.

My Central Park, Gabe thought. *My New York.*

They passed a street musician playing a saxophone. Then they climbed an outcropping of rock.

Gabe pointed to some apartment buildings in the horizon. Their high turrets towered over the green trees.

"See those buildings over there?" Gabe asked. "When I was a little kid I used to pretend they were ships, and that I was fighting them."

"Really?" Rosemary chuckled. "I never took you for a pirate guy."

"I guess I outgrew it," Gabe said with a laugh.

They walked on through Central Park, chatting and laughing all the way. Gabe couldn't believe that a half hour ago he had absolutely nothing to say to Rosemary. Zero. Zip. Zilch. Now he couldn't stop talking!

"I used to practice riding my bike around here,"

Gabe said. "I got wiped out a couple of times. Even lost my training wheels."

"I lost my training wheels here, too," Rosemary said with a smile.

Gabe and Rosemary climbed up Cherry Hill. When they reached the top they gazed down at the lake. With all the trees and flowers in bloom it was the perfect summer day. But to Gabe, any day was perfect when he was with Rosemary.

"See the Boathouse down there?" Rosemary asked. "That's where my aunt is getting married next week."

"Oh, yeah," Gabe remembered. "Flower girl duty."

Rosemary sighed heavily and rolled her eyes.

"Don't remind me," she said. "My aunt asked me to be her flower girl when I was four. Who knew it would take seven years for her boyfriend to pop the question?"

As they reached the path leading back to Mae-Li's birthday party, Gabe made a list of his best qualities. He was charming, suave, and with his unlimited knowledge of Central Park, maybe even fascinating.

Not bad for a first date.

"Maybe we should practice karate some more," Gabe suggested.

"You need it!" Rosemary teased.

"Oh, yeah?" Gabe asked. He held up his hand and spread his fingers wide. "I am this close to becoming a yellow belt."

Rosemary laughed as she spread her arms wide. "Try this close," she said.

"Okay, okay," Gabe said. "What's tomorrow like for you? Maybe we can practice then."

"Saturday?" Rosemary asked. "Um . . . I've got cello lessons in the morning. And in the afternoon I've got tap."

Cello, tap? And karate? How did she keep track of it all?

"What time does tap end?" Gabe asked.

"I'm sorry." Rosemary's dark hair bounced on her shoulders as she shook her head. "After tap I've got this Indian Princess thing I do with my father."

Indian Princess? Gabe couldn't believe it. It was easier scheduling international peace talks than making a date with Rosemary Telesco!

"What's Indian Princess?" Gabe asked.

"It's this 'Daddy and Me' kind of thing," Rosemary explained. "I just do it so my dad won't feel guilty about working late all week."

Okay, Gabe thought calmly. *Let's try again.*

"How about Sunday?" Gabe asked.

"Sunday . . . Sunday . . . Sunday," Rosemary said. She tapped her chin thoughtfully. Then she nodded and said, "Sunday's good."

Gabe could practically hear the angels sing. He had finally found a sliver of free time in Rosemary's super-human schedule!

"Sunday morning?" Gabe asked.

"Can't," Rosemary said, as she shook her head again. "I have to be home in the morning. I have this tutor."

"Tutor?" Gabe asked. "What kind of tutor?"

"To help me pass the tests for private school," Rosemary said. "My parents want me to go to one next year."

"P-private school?" Gabe stammered.

He felt as if someone had kicked him in the gut. Whatever happened to Rosemary's parents believing in the public school system? Rosemary couldn't go to another school. Not now. Not when they were just getting started!

"I probably won't get in anyway," Rosemary said. She smiled slyly at Gabe. "And I can always throw the test."

A weird feeling came over Gabe as he watched Rosemary smile. It was as if the earth moved, ever so slightly.

Whoa! What did that mean? Gabe wondered. *Was that some kind of sign? She'd throw her test for me? Does she like me? Am I supposed to understand all this?*

His thoughts were interrupted by the shouts of a furious nanny: "Rosemary!"

Gabe turned. Birdie was marching up the path with Mae-Li. Her eyes were narrowed and her mouth was a grim line. Definitely not a good sign!

"Uh-oh," Rosemary whispered.

"Where were you, girl?" Birdie demanded. "You almost gave me a heart attack!"

"Sorry, Birdie," Rosemary said. "We were just—"

"—Sorry isn't good enough," Birdie cut in. "You're eleven years old and this is New York City. You can't go off alone. Do you want me to tell your parents on you? Well, do you?"

Something tells me this a good time to leave, Gabe thought.

"I'd better go," Gabe told Rosemary.

"Sunday afternoon, right?" Rosemary asked.

"Yeah!" Gabe said.

"Maybe I should come to your place," Rosemary suggested.

"My place?" Gabe gulped.

He thought about his apartment. Ever since his

dad had moved onto the sofa, he was a little "uninterested" in having friends over. But this wasn't just any friend. It was Rosemary. So he had to face his fears. . . .

"Sounds great," Gabe said.

"See you then," Rosemary said with a little wave.

Gabe watched Rosemary as she walked away with Birdie and Mae-Li. He retrieved his scooter and rode it all the way home. With the wind in his hair and a song in his heart he had never felt so alive. He was young and in the greatest city in the world. And he just had a date with Rosemary Telesco—the third prettiest girl in the class.

No! Gabe thought. *The prettiest girl in the class! The prettiest girl in the whole world!*

Gabe jumped his scooter onto the curb. With Rosemary still on his mind he zoomed up the sidewalk. Until—

Wham! Gabe's scooter clipped some women coming out of a grocery store.

"Hey!" they cried.

As Gabe swerved he nearly hit an old man. The man shook his cane at Gabe and shouted, "Get off the sidewalk, you—you little menace!"

"Sorry!" Gabe called over his shoulder.

Any other day Gabe would have been embarrassed. But nothing could get to him now. He was a man in love. And the world was a beautiful place!

I'm going to see Rosemary on Sunday! Gabe thought as he rolled on. *What day is today? Friday?*

Oh, the eternity!

6

Gabe glided his scooter into his apartment building. The elevator door opened as he crossed the lobby. Ralph grinned as he slid the heavy gate to the side.

"How goes it, Mister Gabe?" Ralph asked. His bald head gleamed under the fluorescent light.

"Pretty fine, Ralph," Gabe said, as he stepped into the elevator.

Real fine!

The gate rattled as Ralph slid it shut. Gabe wondered if Ralph could tell he had just had his first date. From the way his face looked? The way he smelled?

"How's that place kicking treating you?" Ralph asked.

"Place kicking?" Gabe asked. Ever since he had fallen for Rosemary, football had been the last thing on his mind. "I'm really more into karate now."

"Karate?" Ralph asked. "You should check out this TV show, *Extreme Martial Arts with Mike Chat*."

"Mike Chat?" Gabe asked.

"Mike Chat," Ralph repeated.

Gabe made a mental note to watch the show. Did Rosemary know this Mike Chat guy? Did she ever watch *Extreme Martial Arts*?

"Hold the door, please!" a high-pitched voice interrupted his thoughts.

Gabe turned his head. A pretty woman in her early twenties was racing across the lobby toward the elevator. She flipped her long blond hair over her shoulders as she ran. Her high-heeled sandals made clicking noises on the marble floor.

"Don't run, Lina!" Ralph called as he slid the gate back open. "Take your sweet, sweet time."

"Oh, thank you so much, Ralph!" Lina said, as she took her place between Gabe and Ralph.

Gabe noticed that Lina had some kind of accent. What was it? German? Dutch? Russian?

"Hey, no problem, Lina," Ralph said, still grinning. "That's what I'm here for, right?"

The three rode up in silence. Gabe looked sideways at Lina. She was definitely hot. And Ralph was definitely into her. He could tell by the dumb grin on his face. And by the way he kept checking her out.

"Third floor!" Ralph announced as the elevator came to a stop. "Watch your step."

Lina thanked Ralph again as she stepped out. As the elevator moved upward Ralph whispered, "She's the new au pair in Apartment Three-B. From Sweden."

"Sweden," Gabe said with a nod. "Gotcha."

For once in his life Gabe felt a kinship with the balding man who operated the elevator. After all they were both men in love.

That night after dinner Gabe went into the living room. He switched on the TV and found *Extreme Martial Arts with Mike Chat.*

Gabe's eyes popped wide open as he watched Mike Chat spin and kick. This guy was the mack daddy of martial arts!

He stood in front of the TV as he tried to imitate Mike Chat's style. He kicked his foot, careful not to knock over any lamps or plants.

"Ya!" Gabe shouted as he snapped his arms. *"Yee-haaaa!"*

From the corner of his eye he could see his mom and

dad. Leslie was eyeballing him from her computer. Adam was peeking over the arts-and-leisure section of his newspaper. He was watching Gabe, too.

They must think I'm really good, Gabe thought. *Now if I can just convince Rosemary!*

There was something else that Gabe wanted to do for Rosemary. But first it meant a little heart-to-heart talk with his mother.

"Mom?" Gabe asked, later that evening.

Leslie was lying on her bed and reading a fashion magazine. She kept her eyes on the page as she asked, "Yeah, Gabe? What's up?"

"I think I need . . . a haircut," Gabe said.

"A haircut?" Leslie asked.

"Yeah," Gabe said. "A haircut."

"Okay," Leslie said. She licked her finger and turned a page. "I'll do it in the morning."

"You'll . . . do it?" Gabe asked.

He was afraid of that. But what did he expect? Ever since he was a toddler his mom had given him every haircut he had ever had.

Gabe winced as he remembered his mom's less than flattering hairstyles: the bowl cut. The crew cut. The spiked look. They weren't exactly the best haircuts in the world. But then again, mom wasn't exactly a professional haircutter!

I have to ask her sooner or later, Gabe thought. *Better sooner than later.*

Gabe cleared his throat. Leslie looked up from her magazine again.

"Mom, I was thinking," Gabe said. "Maybe I could, um, go out for a haircut?"

Leslie raised an eyebrow and said, "Out?"

"You know, to a barbershop!" Gabe said.

"You mean pay for it?" Leslie cried.

"It doesn't have to be an expensive barbershop, Mom," Gabe said.

Leslie gave a little chuckle. "Don't be ridiculous, honey," she said. "I've been cutting your hair since you were a baby. Just tell me how you want it and I'll cut it that way."

Gabe's jaw dropped. Why didn't his mother get what he was trying to tell her? What part of barbershop did she not understand?

This is getting nowhere! Gabe thought.

He didn't say another word to his mom. Instead, he turned around and walked over to his dad. Adam was spread out on the sofa watching TV.

"Dad!" Gabe said firmly. "I really think it's time

Mom stopped cutting my hair, don't you?"

Adam looked at Gabe. Gabe smiled. He was playing his mom and dad like a true champ!

The next day Gabe got his wish. He sat in the barbershop chair as Vinnie the barber snipped at his hair.

"Let's hope the Yankees win the series this year, right, kid?" Vinnie asked.

"Um, yeah," Gabe said. He tried not to scratch his itchy neck under the towel.

"There's always the Mets," Vinnie went on. "I remember in nineteen eighty-six when the Mets won the series. Man, that game was a nail-biter. Did you ever go to Shea Stadium to watch the Mets?"

Gabe stared at his reflection in the mirror.

"Um . . . can you bring it up just a little more over the ears?" Gabe asked. He had wanted to say that for years!

"Sure," Vinnie said.

After a few more snips Vinnie snapped the towel off.

He picked up a hand mirror and then spun the chair so Gabe could get a roundabout view of his new haircut. His new barbershop haircut!

"So what do you think?" Vinnie asked.

Gabe gave his reflection a satisfied nod. It was the

best twelve dollars Gabe had ever spent. And the best haircut he ever got.

Check me out, Gabe thought with a grin. *I'm hot!*

Gabe walked out of the barbershop feeling like a Gap model. As he headed home he kept glancing at store windows to catch his reflection. What would Rosemary think of his haircut? Would she like it? Would she reach out and run her cool, dainty fingers through it?

Erase! Erase! Gabe thought, thumping his head. How could he have such romantic thoughts when he hadn't even kissed Rosemary yet?

Gabe passed the P.S. 87 basketball court. He saw Max, Sam, and Jacob shooting hoops. They stopped playing when he walked onto the court.

"You look . . . different," Sam said.

"I know," Gabe said. "I just got a haircut."

Max wrinkled his nose. "Why?" he asked. "The first day of school isn't until September."

"You don't have lice, do you?" Jacob asked.

"No!" Gabe said. "I just got a haircut, okay? No big deal."

Gabe picked up the ball and began to dribble. How could he tell his friends the real reason for his barbershop haircut? If they knew he had done it for a girl, he'd be run out of town!

The four friends played a two-on-two game. When it came time for Gabe to go for the hoop, he got fouled by Max. In a flash Gabe was in Max's face.

"Hey!" Gabe shouted. "What're you doing?"

"That was a legitimate foul," Max said.

Gabe pointed his finger at Max's chest. "You totally hacked me," he argued. "I don't need to play with you losers!"

As he stormed off the court Gabe heard Max say, "What's up with him?"

Good question, Gabe thought.

He had never blown up in front of his friends like that before. Could it be some kind of chemical in his new hair gel? Could it be the stress of having a girl in his life? Or could it be that he just wanted to spend time with Rosemary instead of the guys?

Whatever the real reason was, Gabe knew he was changing. But was he changing for the better . . . or for the worse?

Sunday couldn't come quickly enough for Gabe. The first thing he did that morning was straighten up the apartment. He turned the sofa bed back into a sofa. He stuck his dad's stuff neatly in a corner. He even washed the pile of crusty breakfast dishes in the sink.

After a quick lunch of grilled cheese and a glass of milk, it was time to look good for Rosemary. Gabe pulled on a clean T-shirt and jeans. Then he washed his hands and face. After carefully combing his new haircut, he examined himself in the bathroom mirror.

Not bad, Gabe thought. *Cool . . . yet casual.*

Suddenly—*Bzzzzz!*

Gabe dropped the comb in the sink when he heard the buzzer. It was her. It was Rosemary in his lobby!

"Honey, can you see who it is?" Leslie called.

"Got it!" Gabe shouted, a little too loud.

He grabbed the comb and tossed it on the bathroom shelf. He took one last look at himself in the mirror. Then he ran out of the bathroom into the hallway.

"Hello?" Gabe said into the intercom box.

"Hey, Gabe?" Ralph's voice asked. "I got a Rosemary down here for you."

Gabe could hear a faint snicker in Ralph's voice.

"Send her up, Ralph," Gabe said.

He hoped his voice wasn't shaking, like the rest of his body. He opened the door and stared at the elevator.

This is crazy, Gabe thought. *She's a girl, for goodness sake. It's not like she's a New York Knick or something!*

The elevator door slid open. Rosemary stepped out and walked toward Gabe.

"Hi," Rosemary said. "My mom dropped me off. She's going to pick me up at five-fifteen if that's okay."

"Sure," Gabe said. "Whatever."

As Rosemary walked into the apartment Gabe saw Ralph. He was grinning in the elevator and giving a thumbs-up. Gabe blushed. Then he quickly shut the door.

Should I take her jacket? Gabe wondered as they stood in the foyer. *She's not wearing a jacket. Now what?*

Leslie hurried out of her room, fastening an earring. She stopped in her tracks as soon as she saw Rosemary.

"Oh!" Leslie said. She looked surprised to see a girl in the apartment.

"Mom," Gabe said. "You remember Rosemary Telesco, don't you?"

"From kindergarten, of course I do," Leslie said, smiling brightly. "I haven't seen you in ages."

Rosemary smiled politely as Leslie came closer.

"Well, look at you, Rosie!" Leslie said. "You're all grown up."

"Hi, Mrs. Burton," Rosemary said. She shot Gabe

a look that said, "Help!"

"We're practicing karate, Mom," Gabe said quickly. "For our class."

"Terrific," Leslie said, still looking surprised.

The buzzer rang again.

Leslie pressed the button on the intercom and called, "Hello?"

"Ronny's here, Mrs. Burton," Ralph's voice said. "Should I send him up?"

"Yes, thank you, Ralph," Leslie replied.

Gabe groaned under his breath. He had wanted Rosemary's visit to be perfect. And now his mom had a date. A date with obnoxious Ronny!

Could things get any more dysfunctional?

7

"**W**ho's Ronny?" Rosemary whispered.

"My mom's got a date," Gabe muttered.

Leslie put on her lipstick as she waited for Ronny.

"If I knew you were having a play date, Gabe, I wouldn't have made plans," she said. "Should I stay?"

Play date? Gabe thought. *How old does she think I am? Three?*

"It's not a play date, Mom," Gabe explained. "It's karate practice."

"Do you need snacks?" Leslie asked, as she turned in front of the mirror.

"We're fine," Gabe said. "Don't worry about it."

The doorbell rang and Leslie ran to open it. Ronny swaggered inside and kissed her on the cheek. When he saw Gabe, he offered him a high five.

"Hey, big guy!" Ronny said.

"Hey," Gabe said, holding up his hand. He didn't want to high-five Ronny, but he didn't want to be rude in front of Rosemary either.

"Ronny," Leslie said, "this is Gabe's friend Rosemary Telesco."

Ronny turned to Rosemary and smiled. "Nice to meet you Rosemary Telesco!" he said.

"Hi," Rosemary said.

Gabe stood stone-faced. He loved his mom. But why couldn't they just leave already?

"I'll get my jacket," Leslie said, as she ran into her bedroom.

Gabe, Rosemary, and Ronny stood in the foyer. Not a single word was spoken.

Great, Gabe thought. *Is there anything more excruciating than me with my date and Mom's date all hanging out with absolutely nothing to say?*

Suddenly Ronny reached out and ruffled Gabe's hair. His new haircut! "Don't do anything I wouldn't do, kiddo," he said.

That is more excruciating! Gabe thought.

Leslie came back with her jacket and handbag. She gave Gabe a quick kiss on the cheek and said, "I'll be back for dinner."

Gabe watched his mom and Ronny leave the apartment. He was alone with Rosemary at last.

"I didn't know your parents were divorced," Rosemary said.

"They're not officially divorced," Gabe explained. "After a year and a half of waiting for the divorce to be final, my mom decided to move on with her life."

"Too bad," Rosemary said.

"Yeah, well," Gabe said with a shrug.

He didn't really want to talk about his parents. Today was about Rosemary and himself. She was in his apartment—all alone on a Sunday afternoon. And it was time for them to fight!

They moved into the living room and began to practice karate. This time Gabe was totally focused as they sparred. He matched Rosemary's kicks and punches move for move, as if he was channeling the Great One himself. His new master. His new inspiration. Mr. Mike Chat!

It felt so real that Gabe could almost see Mike Chat in his living room talking him through his moves.

"It's a dance, Gabriel," Mike Chat said. "Step. Turn. Kick. You lead her. She doesn't lead you."

Rosemary put up a good fight, but Gabe was

getting better and better. They tussled and then fell to the floor, where they wrestled for a while. Finally Gabe had Rosemary pinned to the carpet. He gazed down at her face.

"Kiss her," a voice whispered into his ear. "Go ahead, Gabe! Kiss her."

"Huh?" Gabe said. He stared over his shoulder at Mike Chat. He knew he was a karate expert. Was he an expert on girls, too?

"That's disgusting!" Gabe hissed. "I can't!"

"Trust me," Mike Chat said with a little smile. "It's not disgusting."

Gabe turned back to Rosemary. He looked deeply into her eyes. She looked deeply into his. Then all of a sudden—

"*Yee-haaaa!*" Rosemary shouted.

Gabe yelped as he felt himself being flipped over. He couldn't believe it. Now Rosemary had him pinned to the ground. How did that happen?

"How could you let her do that?" Mike Chat cried.

Gabe struggled to get up, but it wasn't easy. Rosemary had him pinned under her iron grip!

"Girls . . . mature faster than . . . boys!" Gabe grunted.

"Not true, not true!" Mike Chat exclaimed. "Don't

let her brainwash you into thinking that. Boys are stronger!"

Rosemary's dark hair dangled over Gabe's face as he stared up at her. He had no idea what she was thinking. She was still a total mystery!

What if she kisses me? Gabe wondered. *Do I want to kiss Rosemary?*

The answer was yes. He wanted to. More than anything in the world.

"Um," Gabe said. "Do you want some . . . Gatorade?"

Mike Chat shook his head as he slowly disappeared. Rosemary released Gabe and they both stood up.

The next thing Gabe knew he was standing behind the kitchen counter pouring Gatorade into two glasses.

Who was I kidding? Gabe thought. *Was I really going to kiss her? I mean, come on. She's eleven. I'm ten—well, ten and three quarters actually. Her birthday is in May. Mine is in September.*

Gabe looked up at Rosemary. Her head was inside the refrigerator. "Why are there labels on all the food?" she called out. "What's up with the names?"

"Some of it's my mom's stuff," Gabe explained.

"And some of it's my dad's."

"Wow," Rosemary said, shutting the fridge door. "That must be so hard."

"Not really," Gabe said. "I can take food from either one of them."

"I don't mean the food," Rosemary said. "I mean having them still living together like this."

Gabe just shrugged.

Hey, he thought, *I might be falling in love with the girl. But that doesn't mean I'm in the mood for soul-searching.*

Rosemary climbed up on a stool at the counter. She picked up her glass and took a sip. "Don't you think it's going to be so much better once it's all over?" she asked.

"What do you mean?" Gabe asked.

"You know," Rosemary said. "Once everyone gets on with their lives again."

"I guess so," Gabe admitted.

"Who do you think is going to move out?" Rosemary asked. "Your mom? Or your dad?"

Gabe shrugged as he sipped his drink. He never really thought about that. Probably because he never really wanted to think about it!

"It'll probably be my dad," Gabe said. "That's how

it's supposed to work, right?"

"Right," Rosemary said. She took another sip and then asked, "Has he looked at any apartments yet?"

"Not that I know of," Gabe said.

Rosemary placed down her glass and smiled. "Hey!" she said excitedly. "Maybe we should look for him!"

The Sunday *New York Times* was spread out on the kitchen table. Gabe and Rosemary gathered up the real estate section and carried it into Gabe's bedroom. As they flipped through the pages Rosemary explained her family's favorite hobby: looking at apartments. They didn't actually buy anything, but her parents had been dragging her to open houses for as long as she could remember. So she knew what the ads meant.

"W.B.F.," Rosemary said, as she circled one of the ads with a red pen.

"What does that mean?" Gabe asked.

"Wood-burning fireplace," Rosemary said. "That's a good thing."

"Yeah!" Gabe agreed. He had always wanted a fireplace to roast marshmallows!

Rosemary circled more and more ads. But one really made her excited. "Look at this one," she said, folding back the page. "Romantic treetop view, attic loft, hardwood floors . . ."

Gabe peered over Rosemary's shoulder at the ad. He could smell her strawberry scent . . . or was it the Gatorade on her breath?

"The apartment is a little downtown, but it has two bedrooms," Rosemary went on. "So you can stay over whenever you want."

"Sounds good to me," Gabe said.

"Should we call?" Rosemary asked.

"Call?" Gabe squeaked. She was serious about this, wasn't she? "Okay, let's call."

Gabe dragged the phone into his room. Rosemary dialed the telephone number in the ad.

"Hello?" Rosemary said into the receiver. "Yes, we want to, um, arrange to see the 'romantic treetop view.'"

As Gabe watched Rosemary, he couldn't believe it. She was actually making an appointment with a real estate agent!

Maybe it is true, Gabe thought. *Maybe girls do mature faster than boys.*

Rosemary covered the mouthpiece and whispered, "How's tomorrow afternoon for you?"

"Tomorrow?" Gabe whispered back. "Um, it's good."

"That would be perfect," Rosemary told the real estate agent. "Three o'clock. See you there."

Rosemary hung up the phone just in time. Gabe could hear his dad's keys jangling at the front door.

"I'm home, G-man!" Adam's voice called. "Picked up some kicking tees. Titanium!"

Gabe didn't want his dad to know about the apartment. Not yet. They both stuffed the bulky Sunday *New York Times* under the bed. Then they jumped up and stood side by side.

Adam poked his head in. His eyebrows arched when he saw Rosemary.

"Oh!" Adam said. "How's it going?"

"You remember Rosemary Telesco, right, Dad?" Gabe asked.

"From kindergarten?" Adam asked.

"Hi, Mr. Burton," Rosemary said.

"Hi, Rosemary," Adam said. "Long time, no see."

He shot Gabe a look as if to ask, "What is a girl doing in your room?"

"She's in my karate class, Dad," Gabe said quickly.

But as Gabe walked Rosemary out of the apartment, he knew it was a lot more than that.

Rosemary isn't just in my karate class—she's in my life! Gabe thought. *We're going out to look for an apartment for my dad tomorrow. Those are things boyfriends and girlfriends do.*

Gabe pressed the elevator button. He and Rosemary faced each other as they waited for the elevator to arrive.

What else do boyfriends and girlfriends do? Gabe wondered. The answer came as he gazed at Rosemary.

They kiss!

Gabe stomach did a triple flip. He had survived his first date. He had even survived his first day alone with Rosemary. Would he ever survive his first kiss?

The elevator door slid open, and there was Ralph. Gabe cleared his throat as he snapped back to reality.

"So I'll see you tomorrow," Rosemary said. "Two-thirty."

"Yeah," Gabe said. "See you tomorrow."

Tomorrow, Gabe thought, as he watched Rosemary disappear behind the sliding door. *Are there any more beautiful words in the English language than "See you tomorrow"?*

8

The plan was perfect.

On Monday morning Rosemary would tell her friend Libby to tell Rosemary's parents that she was playing at Libby's house, in case they called. Libby had a grandmother who took care of her. Her grandmother was almost deaf and never heard the phone. So on every front her story was solid.

Gabe would tell his friend Max to do the same thing. There was just one problem. Gabe didn't have the guts to tell Max that he was hanging out with a girl. So he never told him anything!

Luckily Max would be at the skate park that day. Max wouldn't call Gabe's home and ask for him anyway.

So it was all systems go!

Gabe and Rosemary met at two-thirty and headed to the 72nd Street subway station. Gabe swiped his yellow MetroCard in the turnstile. Then he flipped it back to Rosemary and said, "My treat."

Gabe held his scooter as they rode the escalator down to the underground subway platform. He had never ridden his scooter in Greenwich Village before. It would be a first. Just like going all the way downtown without his parents.

After about five minutes the subway rumbled into the station. Gabe and Rosemary stepped inside the car and found two empty seats. They were right next to a teenage couple, their lips locked in a kiss!

As the subway rattled along, Gabe was embarrassed. He tried hard not to look at the teenagers by concentrating on the ads above the windows—ads for plastic surgeons, foot doctors, and Learn-to-Speak-English-in-Three-Weeks schools.

"So . . . um," Gabe said to Rosemary, his eyes still on the ads. "You ever been on the subway without a grown-up before?"

"Actually, um, no," Rosemary said. She was staring up at the ads, too.

"I do it all the time," Gabe said. "It's, you know, much more fun like this."

He didn't have the guts to tell Rosemary the real story—that he had never gone south of West 67th Street before without his mom and dad!

Finally the train reached Christopher Street, their stop. Gabe and Rosemary left the subway car and climbed the stairs out of the station. Gabe looked around the streets of Greenwich Village. He was still in Manhattan, but to him it seemed like another planet.

Where are we? Gabe wondered.

The street signs made absolutely no sense. Instead of having numbers like the signs uptown, they had names like Bleecker, Greenwich, Carmine, and Jane.

"We want to go to Grove Street," Rosemary said, studying the ad. "That's where the building is."

Gabe pushed his scooter through the crowded narrow streets. The buildings were smaller than those uptown. And the stores sold a lot of leather and silver jewelry. The people in the Village looked kind of different, too. Lots of them wore black. Some had wild-colored hair and piercings.

"I think we got off a stop early," Gabe said. He nodded toward the back of his scooter. "Do you want to . . . ?"

Rosemary looked down at the scooter. "You think

we can?" she asked. "I mean . . . both of us?"

"We could try," Gabe said.

Rosemary hopped onto the scooter. As she wrapped her arms around Gabe's middle, he felt exhilarated.

"Hold on!" Gabe said. He kicked his scooter forward. With the two of them on board it swayed side to side. Keeping his balance was tricky, but Gabe got the hang of it. Soon they were riding up and down the streets of the Village—together!

On Barrow Street Gabe veered around a woman walking a poodle. He weaved in and out of the crowd on Commerce Street. But when Gabe found himself back on Christopher and Bleecker, he knew they had gone around in a complete circle!

"Maybe you should ask directions," Rosemary suggested.

"No!" Gabe said. He pointed between two small buildings. "I think Grove Street is just down this alley."

Rosemary threw back her head and laughed out loud. "You are so like all the guys in my family," she said. "You never want to ask directions."

Rosemary hopped off the scooter and ran into a store. Gabe stood on the sidewalk watching her through the glass window. She was already chatting with the storekeeper as though she knew him all her life.

Look at her, Gabe thought. *So confident. So sure of herself. So . . . so . . . amazing!*

"That your girl?" a voice snapped.

"Huh?" Gabe asked, spinning around.

Standing behind him was a street vendor. He was holding a tray of bogus designer watches. His hair was stringy, his jacket was stained, and a long thin scar streaked down his cheek like a rusty zipper.

The guy nodded toward the store and asked again, "Is that your girl?"

My girl! Gabe thought with a slow smile. *I think I can get used to hearing that.*

"Yeah," Gabe said proudly. "That's my girlfriend."

The guy glanced over both shoulders. Then he leaned over to Gabe and began to whisper. "I had a girlfriend once upon a time, too. She trampled my heart and left me bleeding on the floor."

"R-really?" Gabe stammered.

"Run!" the guy hissed.

"Um." Gabe gulped. "Excuse me?"

He could see Rosemary leaving the store.

"Run while you still can, brother!" the guy said.

"Take my advice. Make like the wind!"

The guy straightened up. Then he went back to hawking his watches.

Who was that creepy guy? Gabe wondered.

He was still wondering when Rosemary walked over.

"Grove Street isn't too far," Rosemary said. "It's one block, a left, and another left."

She hopped behind Gabe and held his waist. Gabe pushed off and glanced back. The scary-looking guy was eyeballing him and shaking his head.

Too weird! Gabe thought.

He turned his attention back to the road ahead of him. When they reached Grove Street, the cement street turned into cobblestones. Gabe's teeth rattled as the scooter bumped down the street. Rosemary held him tighter.

"There it is," Rosemary said, pointing over Gabe's shoulder. "There's the building."

Gabe stopped the scooter in front of a tidy little brownstone. A man wearing a suit was standing on the stoop, studying his watch. He didn't look at Gabe and Rosemary as they climbed the steps.

"Are you Issac?" Rosemary called.

The man wrinkled his brow in confusion. "Yeah," he said slowly, "but—"

"I'm Rosemary."

Issac stared at Gabe and Rosemary. Then he grinned and said, "Okay, am I getting punked?"

"We're here to look at the apartment," Rosemary said in a firm voice.

"Newlyweds?" Issac joked.

Gabe ignored the crack. "It's for my dad!" he said.

"Oh, really?" Issac said. "And will Daddy be meeting us here?"

"He will if I give him the high sign," Gabe said bravely. "Are you trying to make a commission or not?"

Gabe couldn't believe it. He actually spoke up for himself. Could Rosemary's confidence be rubbing off on him?

Issac stood silently on the stoop. Finally he sighed and unlocked the front door. Gabe and Rosemary exchanged grins as they followed him into the brownstone.

We did it! Gabe thought.

The vacant apartment was on the top floor. As they walked through the door the shiny hardwood floors squeaked under their feet.

"A lot of divorced fathers buy two-bedroom apartments," Issac said.

Gabe liked the apartment. It was big and had a lot of windows. But he didn't like the idea of his dad moving out, even if he would have his own attic loft.

"So what do you think, Gabe?" Rosemary asked.

Gabe stared out a window at the treetop view. It was romantic, just like the ad said. The most romantic treetop view Gabe had ever seen.

"Nice," Gabe said. "Real nice."

He turned to look at Rosemary. She was smiling, too. Her cheeks were flushed.

"This place is going to be gone in a New York minute," Issac cut in. "I promise you."

"Thank you, Issac," Rosemary said. "We'll be in touch."

Gabe and Rosemary walked out of the brownstone. They had accomplished their mission. They had come downtown by themselves and had seen the apartment. Now it was time to leave the Village and go home.

"I have an idea," Gabe said, as they climbed back on the scooter. "Let's take this all the way uptown."

"All the way uptown?" Rosemary gasped. "That's more than sixty blocks!"

"I know!" Gabe said with a grin.

Rosemary's eyes flashed as she considered the adventure. Then she hopped aboard and said, "Go for it!"

Gabe took the scooter up the bike path along the Hudson River. It was the most physically grueling experience of Gabe's ten years on this planet. But with Rosemary on board Gabe hardly felt his aching muscles. All he felt was joy!

Gabe huffed and puffed as he kicked his scooter northward. They passed the warehouses of the West 30s. The parking structures of the West 50s. And finally the high-rise buildings of the West 60s.

As Gabe rode, he watched his city go by.

This is New York the way I want to remember it, Gabe thought with grin. *The place where anything is possible. City of dreams!*

The sun was just going down as Gabe and Rosemary turned off the bike path into their neighborhood. As Gabe wearily scooted down 71st Street, Rosemary pointed to a small park between two buildings.

"What's that?" Rosemary asked.

Gabe circled back around. "You don't know about this?" he asked. "It's the smallest park in the city."

"Cool," Rosemary said. "Let's go in."

Gabe and Rosemary hopped off the scooter. After Gabe stood on his scooter for so long, his legs felt kind of wobbly.

He led Rosemary through the iron gate into the tiny park. It was small but wide enough for a stone path lined with neatly trimmed bushes. In the back was a single bench.

"How come I didn't know about this park?" Rosemary asked, looking around. "It's great."

"No one who lives on your side of Broadway ever comes over here," Gabe said. "That's what's so cool about West End Avenue."

Gabe looked into Rosemary's eyes. She didn't look away. Pigeons cooed and crickets chirped as the two of them stood gazing into each other's eyes.

What am I waiting for? Gabe wondered. *If I'm ever going to kiss a single girl in my whole entire life, why not now? Who cares if I'm only ten and three quarters?*

He was about to move in toward Rosemary when—

"Hey!" a voice growled. "What are you doing in my park?"

Gabe's and Rosemary's heads snapped around.

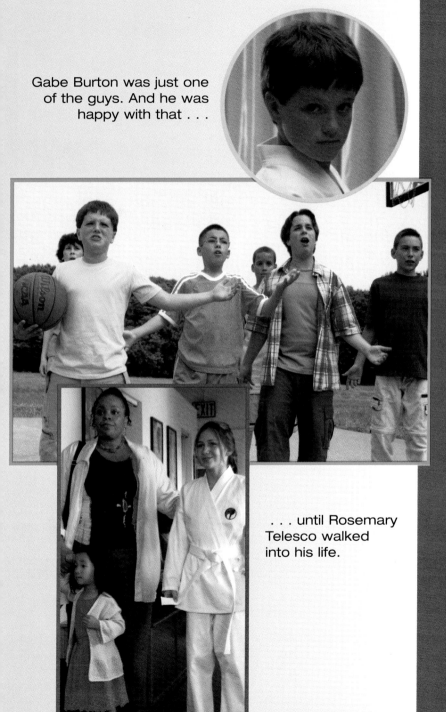

Gabe Burton was just one of the guys. And he was happy with that . . .

. . . until Rosemary Telesco walked into his life.

Maybe they could just be friends.

But how could Gabe resist a girl this beautiful?

Gabe has a thing or two to learn about karate and girls.

Rosemary breaks the news: Their days are numbered. She's off to summer camp in just a few short weeks.

Gabe and Rosemary explore Manhattan.

New York is a whole different city when you have someone to share it with.

Rosemary is assigned a new sparring partner.

Gabe finally makes his move.

Gabe comes face-to-face with his competition,
Tim Staples.

So much for impressing Rosemary . . .

A wounded, jealous Gabe can't take it anymore and tells Rosemary he hates her.

Love is pure agony!

Gabe makes it to the wedding just in time for the last dance.

There sitting on his bike and blocking the narrow path was the monster of P.S. 87! The only thirteen-year-old in the fifth grade—Daryl Kitzens!

Gabe felt his blood turn to ice.

Oh, no, he thought. *Not here. Not now!*

9

"**I** said, what are you doing in my park?" Daryl demanded.

Gabe gulped.

Rosemary folded her arms across her chest. She stuck out her chin and said, "It's a public park!"

Gabe stared at Rosemary. What was she doing? Didn't she know that wild animals needed to be soothed—not provoked?

Daryl climbed off his bike. He laid it across the pathway and inched his way toward Gabe and Rosemary.

Gabe stepped in front of Rosemary. He wanted to protect her. He wanted to protect himself, too!

"H-hey, um," Gabe stammered. "This park is big enough for all of us, right?"

A dark shadow loomed over Gabe as Daryl towered over him. He could feel his knees knocking together.

Mike Chat! Where are you when I need you?

Gabe tried to find his karate stance, but Daryl shoved him in the chest. He bounced back hard against Rosemary.

Who are we kidding? Gabe thought. *A white belt and a yellow belt facing off against the terror of P.S. 87? We're going to get creamed!*

Suddenly Rosemary darted out from behind Gabe and—*Wham!*

Gabe stared in disbelief. Rosemary had just kicked Daryl right in the gut!

"Ooowwww!" Daryl cried as he doubled over.

Without thinking Gabe leaped forward. His hands became a blur as he karate-chopped Daryl in the face!

"Yaaa!" Gabe cried as he chopped away.

"Hee-yaaa!" Rosemary shouted as she kicked.

Daryl tried to fight back. But the swift chops and kicks were too much for him. Soon the biggest bully in the neighborhood was down for the count.

Gabe picked up his scooter. He and Rosemary jumped over Daryl's bike and raced out of the park. They climbed onto the scooter and took off. Gabe thought they were safe until he looked back and saw

Daryl chasing them on his bike!

Kicking his foot furiously, Gabe picked up speed. Soon he was scooting across Broadway with Daryl on his tail. Gabe thought he was a goner. Until the terror of P.S. 87 got lost in a wave of oncoming traffic!

"We lost him." Rosemary sighed with relief.

Gabe was relieved, too, but he wasn't taking any chances. He rode his scooter along side streets and didn't slow down until he reached Rosemary's building.

"Well," Rosemary said, stepping off the scooter. "Good night."

"Good night," Gabe said.

Again they looked into each other's eyes.

Why can't I do it? Gabe thought. *I can fight off Daryl Kitzens. So why can't I kiss Rosemary?*

"That was fun," Rosemary said.

Do it, you wimp, Gabe thought. *Just do it.*

But instead . . .

"Yeah," Gabe blurted. "It was."

"Are you scared Daryl will hunt us down?" Rosemary asked.

Gabe shook his head. "I'll just keep a low profile for the rest of the summer," he said. "Then transfer to military school in the fall."

Rosemary giggled. "I'll just have to keep a low profile for one more week," she said.

"A week?" Gabe asked. "What do you mean?"

"Next Sunday, after my aunt's wedding, I'm going to camp," Rosemary said.

Did she just say camp? Gabe thought.

The word felt like a dagger through Gabe's heart! Rosemary couldn't be going away to camp. Not her. Not now! Maybe it was just day camp. Or a weekend camping trip. Yeah, that's it!

"For how long?" Gabe asked casually.

"Six weeks," Rosemary answered. "The camp is up in Maine."

Six weeks? That was even longer than a month! And Maine was practically Canada!

Gabe groaned under his breath. Rosemary may as well have said she was moving away for good!

"Wow," Gabe said, forcing a smile. "That's fantastic."

"Yeah," Rosemary said. After looking into his eyes for another few seconds, she finally said, "I'd better go inside."

Gabe said good night to Rosemary as she walked under the awning into her building. He had missed another chance to kiss her!

What if she goes to camp and I never kiss her? Gabe wondered, as he rode his scooter home. *Every opportunity I have will go the same way—"Good night," "Good night."*

Gabe felt himself panic. *I will not let that happen!* he decided. *I will kiss her before she gets on that bus to Maine. I will! I will! I will!*

Gabe glided his scooter up his block. He slowed down when he saw police cars with flashing lights right in front of his building.

What's going on? Gabe wondered.

Gabe rolled his scooter through the front door. A bunch of police officers were talking to Ralph in the lobby. When Ralph turned toward Gabe, he smiled with relief.

Uh-oh, Gabe thought. *I have a feeling all this is about me!*

Gabe was right. Max had gotten sick so he hadn't gone to the skate park. Gabe's mom had run into Max's mom at the supermarket. And the rest was history. . . .

"Don't you ever go anywhere without us knowing where you are!" Leslie sobbed as Gabe walked through the door. "You worried us half to death!"

Adam stepped into the foyer. The frown on his face

told Gabe he was in deep trouble.

And he was. No phone. No TV. No leaving the apartment for forty-eight hours!

Leslie agreed with the sentence. It was the first thing Gabe's parents had agreed on in years!

Forty-eight hours? Gabe thought.

He quickly did the math inside his head. Forty-eight hours was two whole days. If he couldn't leave the apartment, he couldn't go to karate class—and if he couldn't go to karate class, he couldn't see Rosemary!

Gabe spent the whole night trying to revoke his sentence. But his mom was a tough nut to crack.

"Please, Mom!" Gabe begged. *"Pleeeease?"*

"I told you over and over," Leslie said. "It's non-negotiable. It's not what you did, it's not telling me—"

"I know, I know!" Gabe cut in. "I'm sorry. But—"

"Do I have to call Rosemary's mother?" Leslie asked. "And tell her what you both did today?"

Gabe gasped. Calling Rosemary's parents would be a fate worse than death!

"No!" Gabe said. "Please—don't call anyone!"

Leslie folded her arms across her chest. "I thought we were all clear about the area you're free to roam," she said. "We need to know you're safe."

Gabe had no choice. If he was going to get permission to go to karate class and see Rosemary, he had to throw himself upon the mercy of the court. He dropped to his knees and grabbed his mom's hand. Then he began to wail:

"I will wash dishes for the entire summer if you let me go to karate. I promise! I promise! I promise!"

In a flash, Gabe was in the kitchen scrubbing a towering stack of greasy plates, pots, and pans.

This was no light sentence. The steam from the hot water made his nose run. The yellow plastic gloves itched. The crusty tomato sauce on the dishes had to be practically chiseled off.

But it was better than forty-eight hours of house arrest. And a few dishes were a small price to pay to see Rosemary once more before she disappeared for six weeks.

By the time Gabe fell into bed he was exhausted. He had ridden his scooter sixty eight blocks, fought off a bully, and washed a mother lode of dirty dishes. Now he was about to listen to an interminable lecture from his dad.

"You really gave us a scare today," Adam said, as he tucked Gabe into bed.

"I know," Gabe said. "I'm sorry."

"Think you learned your lesson?" Adam asked.

Gabe nodded. He still hadn't told his dad the real reason he and Rosemary went downtown. Maybe it was time.

"Dad?" Gabe asked. "Are you going to move out?"

Adam sat down on the bed.

"Eventually," Adam said. Then he nodded. "Yeah, I am, Gabe."

Gabe sat up straight. "Okay," he said, "because I found you an apartment today."

"You found me an apartment?" Adam exclaimed.

"That's where I went today," Gabe said. "To look for an apartment for you."

"You want me to move out, Gabe?" Adam asked.

"No!" Gabe said, shaking his head. "But maybe we can all get our lives started again after you move out."

Adam laughed as he stroked Gabe's hair off his forehead. "Where do you get such big ideas?" he asked.

"I just get them," Gabe said.

"Okay." Adam sighed. "What's this apartment like?"

"It's a two-bedroom apartment," Gabe explained. "And it's on Grove Street."

"Isn't that in the Village?" Adam asked.

Gabe nodded. "It has an attic loft," he went on. "And a wood-burning fireplace—"

"Can't do it," Adam interrupted.

"Why not?" Gabe asked.

"It's too far from you, boss," Adam said. "I wouldn't move more than three or four blocks away from you."

"Really?" Gabe asked.

"Really," Adam said. "In fact, you're going to have to go to college to get any farther away from me."

Gabe smiled as he snuggled back under the covers. Having his dad three or four blocks away was way better than an attic loft.

"So," Adam said, standing up. "What's up with that Rosemary?"

"Rosemary?" Gabe asked coolly. "What do you mean?"

"Nothing," Adam said. "I'm just not used to seeing you with a girl."

"We do karate together, Dad," Gabe insisted. "We're sparring partners."

Adam pressed his lips together as he nodded. "Oh," he said. "Okay."

"I didn't even pick her," Gabe added. "We were the

only ones in the class without partners. So we didn't have a choice."

"Hey, whatever you say, champ," Adam said. He turned off the light as he left the room.

Gabe was so wiped out, he fell asleep instantly. He also had the strangest dream. . . .

"Watch your step," Ralph said as he opened the elevator door.

Gabe stepped out. He wasn't in the lobby. Or on the eighth floor. He was on a basketball court!

Max was there. So were Sam and Jacob. Gabe ran over to join them. Soon they were playing two on two. But everything was in slow motion, the way things sometimes are in dreams.

As Gabe shot the ball toward the basket, he saw Rosemary. She was sitting on the grass at the end of the court. She was reading a book and wearing her fancy blue flower-girl dress.

She looks like a dream! Gabe thought. *Hey, wait a minute. This is a dream!*

"Check it up, dude!" Sam said, shooting the ball to Gabe. "Check it up!"

Gabe caught the ball. He turned it around in his hands, his eyes still on Rosemary.

Which way do I go? Gabe thought. *To the hoop. Or to Rosemary?*

"Come on, man!" Max called. "It's thirteen all."

Gabe stared at his friends. They looked weird and distorted. Like in those funhouse mirrors at Coney Island.

He began dribbling the ball. Suddenly he began to separate into two Gabes—one Gabe played basketball, the other Gabe ran across the court toward Rosemary!

"What are you doing?" the basketball-playing Gabe began to shout. "Get back here! She's gross! We're in the middle of a point, man!"

The other Gabe kept on running. Rosemary looked up from her book and smiled. She stood up and began running toward Gabe, too. When the two came together they hugged. Then they began to twirl around and around and around until they were floating twenty feet high in the air!

"Rosemary," Gabe mumbled in his sleep. "Rosemary."

It was one of the weirdest dreams Gabe ever had. It was also one of the best!

The next morning Gabe felt on top of the world. For some reason the weird dream made him love Rosemary even more.

As he bounded up the stairs to his karate class, Gabe couldn't wait to see Rosemary. He couldn't wait to grapple with her and smell her strawberry-scented hair.

But once in the studio, Gabe heard the words that would ruin his life. . . .

"We're going to switch sparring partners today," Master Coles announced, "to make sure everyone's working with their level."

Switch . . . partners? Gabe thought.

He and Rosemary shared worried looks. Neither one of them wanted to switch partners, especially Gabe.

"Rosemary," Master Coles said. "From now on, you'll be with Tim Staples."

Gabe turned to look at Tim. The big guy had just gotten a yellow belt just like Rosemary's. He was able to break through a half-inch board with his fist. He was also the tallest and best-looking guy in the whole class. Maybe even the whole borough!

Oh, no! Gabe thought, breaking into a sweat. *Nooooo!*

Gabe's stomach churned as he watched Rosemary join Tim. The two smiled at each other and nodded.

They may not be in love yet, but give it time, Gabe thought angrily. *Soon they'll date. Then they'll get engaged. Then, married. And where will I be? I'll be the loser standing outside the church pounding on the glass door!*

"Gabe," Master Coles said. "Your partner will be David Betanahu."

Gabe turned to look at David. He was a scrawny little kid with fuzzy facial hair and sweat stains under his arms. He was also a white belt.

This is my level? Gabe thought. *David Betanahu?*

He looked in Rosemary's direction. She was busy smiling and chatting with Tim.

Rosemary is with the teen idol, Gabe thought glumly.

And I'm with the sweatiest ten-year-old in Manhattan!

Gabe could see David's mom sitting with the other mothers and nannies. She had a moustache, too!

It must run in the family, Gabe thought. *David's had a moustache since kindergarten!*

As they sparred, Gabe tried to keep David from sweating all over him. He could see Rosemary in the mirror as they circled. She and Tim were sparring together like pros!

Everything I took for granted, Gabe thought. *Stolen. In a New York minute.*

Wham!

Gabe gasped as David flipped him onto the mat. He stared up at the ceiling and heaved a big sigh. Life wasn't quite the same without Rosemary. Not the same at all.

The rest of the class was unbearable. David was sweating more and more profusely with every passing minute. And Gabe couldn't keep his eyes off Rosemary.

When the class was over, Gabe walked outside with Rosemary. Birdie and Mae-Li were behind them as usual.

"How did that go for you?" Gabe asked. "Good class for you?"

"I'm having trouble with this *mai te zuki* maneuver," Rosemary admitted.

Gabe raised an eyebrow. Rosemary not only was sparring like a pro, she was starting to sound like one, too!

"So am I," Gabe said. "How's that Tim guy with the *mai te zuki*?"

I can't believe I asked her that, Gabe thought. *What am I trying to do, torture myself?*

"Tim is a lot better than me," Rosemary said. "He wants us to practice together."

Practice together? That meant spending time together! Gabe wanted to gag as he imagined Tim eating cookies in Rosemary's kitchen and sparring with Rosemary in her strawberry-scented room. But all he could say was, "R-really? That's . . . terrific."

They walked on in silence, until Gabe asked, "So when should we get together?"

"Well," Rosemary said slowly, "I've got cello this afternoon."

"I thought cello was on Saturday," Gabe said.

"Tuesday and Saturday," Rosemary reminded.

Gabe frowned. Couldn't Rosemary cancel her stupid cello lesson? Didn't she know their days were numbered before she got on that bus to Maine?

"Um," Rosemary said. "How about . . . if I call you?"

"Sure," Gabe said. "That sounds . . . great."

He stood at the corner while Rosemary, Birdie, and Mae-Li crossed the street.

So that's it? Gabe wondered. *We spent a whole day together on a scooter and all I've got to show for it is a lousy "call you?"*

What did that mean? When would Rosemary call him? What day? What time?

That night Gabe sat in the kitchen next to the answering machine. He hit the play button for about the fifteenth time.

"You have no new messages," the voice on the machine announced.

"Rats," Gabe muttered. He rested his chin on the kitchen counter and sighed. How could he go on without Rosemary? How could he go back to living his old miserable life?

He remembered shooting hoops with Max, Sam, and Jacob. He was happy once. Or at least he thought he was happy. He just didn't know he was miserable yet.

So the next day Gabe returned to his old drill: kicking field goals with his dad in Riverside Park.

"G-man," Adam said. "Where's your head today?"

"My head?" Gabe asked, after he shanked the ball all the way to the left.

"It's not with the ball," Adam said. "What kind of a kick was that?"

Gabe gazed into the distance. He couldn't tell his dad about Rosemary. Why should he? It was over.

"It's not my head, Dad," he said. "It's just my leg."

"Your leg?" Adam asked.

"Um, yeah!" Gabe said quickly. "I hurt it kind of bad in karate class."

"I warned you about karate, didn't I?" Adam said. "It has nothing to do with being a place kicker. We have to keep our priorities in line."

Gabe nodded. His dad was right. His priorities were all messed up.

I am an athlete, Gabe thought. *I have to shake off these dumb feelings about a girl!*

After dinner Gabe sat in the living room playing Street Fighter on his PlayStation. He smiled as he kicked the lights out of a tall, blond handsome street fighter, who looked kind of like Tim Staples.

Look at me! Gabe thought as he played. *I can bounce back. I don't need some girl in my life to be happy!*

As Gabe jabbed the buttons on the keypad, he made up his mind to spend more time with Max, Sam, and Jacob. After all, girlfriends come and go, but best buds were forever!

The phone rang. Gabe looked up from his game as his dad answered it.

Is it Rosemary? Gabe wondered. *Is it?*

But then he heard his dad say, "Sorry. We don't take marketing calls. Thank you."

Gabe's heart plummeted as he went back to his game. Maybe he wasn't bouncing back as well as he thought. He didn't bother looking up when the phone rang a few minutes later.

"Gabe!" Adam called. "It's for you."

"Me?" Gabe asked.

Adam was holding the phone out for him.

"It's a girl," he said with a smile.

Before he could say *mai te zuki*, Gabe was hurrying into his room with the phone. He shut the door behind him, cupped the mouthpiece with his hand, and shouted, "Got it!"

Gabe waited until he heard a click. He took a deep breath, uncupped the mouthpiece, and said, "Hi."

"I said I was going to call," Rosemary said.

"Did you?" Gabe asked. "I don't even remember."

Smooth under pressure. That's how Gabe wanted to sound. Now if only he could do something about his hammering heart!

"So what are you doing tomorrow night?" Rosemary asked.

"Tomorrow night?" Gabe asked.

"It's summer, so it's not a school night or anything," Rosemary added.

Gabe bit his lip. Was Rosemary asking him out?

Okay. Don't act too psyched, Gabe told himself. *Smooth and cool all the way.*

"I'm free," he blurted. "Sure. Totally."

"My parents have these tickets to this concert with this guy who's supposed to be the greatest singer in New York or something," Rosemary explained. "They were going to take my aunt who's getting married, but she and my mom got in this big fight. So, do you want to go?"

"Me and your parents?" Gabe asked.

It was too uncanny for words. A few hours ago he and Rosemary were history. Now he was meeting the parents!

"And me too, of course," Rosemary added. "My mom said she'd talk to your mom."

A conversation between the mothers, Gabe thought.

This is *getting serious!*

Gabe thought about the concert. He didn't have a clue who this singer was. And he didn't care!

"Sounds awesome!" Gabe said.

"Okay," Rosemary said. "See you tomorrow."

Gabe hung up the phone. He stood up and pumped his fist in the air. "Ye-es!" he cheered under his breath. Rosemary was back in his life. And it felt great!

Unless, Gabe thought, *this is a dream, too.*

Gabe shook his head. This was not just some figment of his imagination. Their love was a two-way street.

And all the signs pointed ahead!

"**L**ooking sharp there, tiger," Leslie said.

It was the night of the concert. Gabe came out of his room wearing his only suit. His hair was slicked with hair gel.

"Like I even care," Gabe snorted.

He couldn't let on how he really felt. How he wanted Rosemary to take one look at him and totally melt!

Tim Staples, step aside!

"I especially like the hair," Adam said.

Gabe glanced at his reflection in the mirror. Was there something wrong with his hair? Did it look too neat? Too messy?

"Why don't you muss it up a little?" Adam suggested.

Leslie groaned and shook her head. "Don't get all

your romantic guidance from him, Gabe," she said. "You look very nice."

Gabe mussed his hair just a bit. It did look better.

"I'm going to wait downstairs," Gabe said.

"Want us to say hi to her parents?" Leslie asked.

"Nope," Gabe said.

"They promised you'd be back by eleven," Leslie said, walking him to the door. "If you're going to be one second later, I need a call."

"Okay," Gabe said.

He left the apartment and pressed the elevator button. Ralph stopped on his floor and slid the gate aside.

"Pretty snazzy!" Ralph said. "Big night?"

"Just a date," Gabe said. "With this, you know, girl. No big deal."

"The girl who came by the other day?" Ralph asked.

Gabe nodded. He felt like a proud peacock!

"She was a nice girl!" Ralph exclaimed. "All right, Mister Gabe!"

When the elevator touched down in the lobby, Gabe said good-bye to Ralph. As he left the building he saw a yellow taxi pulling up. The back door opened, and Mickey Telesco hurried out. As Mickey ran to the front, Gabe slipped into the backseat right next to Rosemary. Her mom, Jackie, leaned over and smiled.

"Glad you could join us, Gabe," Jackie said.

"Thanks," Gabe said. "Me too."

After Gabe clicked on his seatbelt and smiled at Rosemary, the taxi took off. It whisked them through Central Park to a fancy hotel on the Upper East Side. A doorman hurried over to open the taxi door. Gabe and the Telescos stepped out.

As they strolled toward the entrance Gabe spotted a sign that read "Loston Harris Live at the Carlyle." So that's who they were seeing!

They made their way across the lobby and into the hotel lounge. A maitre d' led them to a table near the stage. Mr. and Mrs. Telesco sat in chairs. Gabe and Rosemary sat next to each other on the loveseat.

"You kids are going to love this guy," Mr. Telesco told them. "Jackie and I saw him here three years ago. No one sings like Loston Harris. This guy is New York!"

Piano music filled the lounge as the lights went down. Loston Harris walked onto the stage to wild cheers and applause. The audience cheered even louder when Loston broke into his first song, "To Be Determined." It was a song about love. About a boy and a girl, and how the boy could think of nothing but holding the girl's hand.

Gabe glanced sideways at Rosemary. He could see her hand resting on the seat beside him. He didn't have the guts to take it. But as Gabe listened to the song he knew their relationship had to get to the next step, or they would just stay karate friends forever!

Okay, Gabe thought. *Go for it. Just go for it.*

Gabe swallowed hard. He let his hand fall onto Rosemary's. He felt her fingers closing around his own.

I can't believe it! Gabe thought. *We're holding hands. We're actually holding hands!*

Gabe wanted the moment to last forever. He wanted to hold Rosemary's hand for the rest of the show, for the rest of the night. Even if their hands were getting kind of sweaty.

Suddenly Rosemary grabbed her hand back. Her eyes stayed focused on the stage as she wiped her hand on her pant leg.

What does this mean? Gabe thought, horrified. *Does she hate me? Is she grossed out? Am I pushing everything too fast?*

But then Rosemary took Gabe's hand again. His heart soared. They held hands all through the show, only letting go to applaud Loston after each song.

After the concert another taxi drove them home.

"You're so quiet, Jackie," Mickey said from the front seat. "Didn't you like the show?"

"I just feel bad," Jackie said. "We got the tickets for my sister. She's the one who loves Loston Harris so much. We shouldn't be fighting about petty things the week of her wedding."

"I have an idea, Mom," Rosemary said. "Why don't you ask Loston Harris to sing for Aunt Colleen at her wedding?"

"Yeah, right!" Jackie scoffed.

"I'm serious, Mom!" Rosemary said. "You're in show business. Loston Harris is in show business."

"I know, Rosie," Jackie said. "But people in show business have a silent agreement not to ask other people in show business to sing at their weddings."

Mickey laughed. "Do you know how long it took just to get these tickets?" he asked. "Our agent had to call all over town!"

As the taxi made its way to the Upper West Side, Gabe smiled out the window. He was dating the daughter of show-business people. In New York City that was practically royalty!

He watched people sauntering along the streets of

Manhattan. They almost seemed as if they were dancing.

Hey, wait a minute, Gabe thought. *They are dancing!*

The city streets outside had turned into one big splashy Broadway musical. Men and women were spinning and dipping and singing their hearts out!

Gabe knew the dance number was a fantasy. But who cared? His life was becoming one happy love song—where boy met girl, girl met boy, and romance was in the air!

The taxi came to a stop in front of Gabe's building. Mickey climbed out first. He held the back door as Gabe, Rosemary, and Jackie stepped out. It was such a nice summer night that the Telescos decided to walk home.

"You two say good night now," Jackie told Rosemary. "Daddy and I are going into the deli to buy some milk."

"Good night, Mrs. Telesco," Gabe said politely. "And thanks."

"Thank you for coming, Gabe," Jackie said.

Gabe waited until Rosemary's parents were in the deli. Then he turned to Rosemary and said, "Your parents are really cool."

"Everybody says I'm going to hate them when I get older," Rosemary said.

"Do you think you will?" Gabe asked.

"Probably," Rosemary said. "If people say so."

The two stood silently in front of Gabe's building. *This is it*, Gabe thought. *I know it. She knows it. Her parents know it. Why can't I kiss her? What's stopping me? Fear of cooties?*

Rosemary gave a little shrug and said, "Big wedding this weekend."

"Oh, yeah," Gabe said. "Right."

"I wish you could come with me," Rosemary said. "It's going to be so boring."

"I'd like to see you do your flower girl stuff," Gabe said, staring at Rosemary's lips.

"Don't remind me," Rosemary said. "I'm so afraid I'm going to—"

Gabe lunged forward and planted a kiss on Rosemary's mouth. It felt weird but nice. When Gabe was finished he backed away. He couldn't look Rosemary in the eyes. He had a feeling she couldn't look at him either.

Did I do it right? Gabe wondered, his eyes darting up and down. *I don't know. I have absolutely nothing to compare it to. Was I even close?*

Rosemary shuffled her feet nervously as her parents walked out of the deli.

"I have to go," Rosemary said.

"Me too," Gabe said. "Good night."

Rosemary hurried over to her parents.

Gabe stood alone on the sidewalk watching the Telescos walk away. He had finally kissed Rosemary. So why did he feel so . . . confused?

He entered his building in a daze and rode up the elevator with Ralph.

"So how was your concert, little Romeo?" Ralph teased.

"Good!" Gabe blurted. "Great, I think."

That night in bed Gabe lay wide awake. He couldn't stop thinking about the kiss. His first kiss. Did Rosemary want him to kiss her? Or did he scare her away? Was it too fast? Too sloppy? Too gross?

Gabe sat up straight in bed. He had this funky feeling in the pit of his stomach. He knew it wasn't something he ate. And it wasn't flu season. It was a case of lovesickness—and he had it bad!

Jumping out of bed, Gabe raced to the bathroom. He kneeled over the toilet and began to barf.

Maybe this is what cooties are, Gabe thought in between hurls. After throwing up for a good five

105

minutes, Gabe heard a knock on the door.

"Gabe?" Adam called through the door. "Are you all right in there?"

Gabe leaned against the tile wall to catch his breath. Then he called out, "I'm okay, Dad."

But he really wasn't.

The next morning Gabe was still a wreck. He finally had Rosemary's number, but he couldn't call her. Except for the time he phoned and hung up. Instead Gabe waited until it was time for karate class. He would see Rosemary and take it from there.

Gabe carried his scooter up the stairs to the karate studio. He was ten minutes early, but he wasn't alone. Master Coles was there. So was Tim Staples.

"Hey," Gabe said to Tim.

"Hey," Tim said back.

Gabe stayed on one side of the studio and Tim stayed on the other. When Tim started doing stretching exercises, so did Gabe.

Why is he here so early? Gabe wondered.

He imagined his white belt magically transforming to yellow. Then he imagined himself walking up to Tim and punishing him with a series of furious chops and jabs.

If only life were so easy, Gabe thought with a sigh.

A few minutes later the class was in full swing. Everyone was there except Rosemary. Gabe looked at the clock on the wall and frowned.

Three-oh-nine, he thought. *She's not even coming. She doesn't even want to see me. She's blowing off class. She hates me!*

Gabe was about to panic when the door swung open. Rosemary rushed in with Birdie and Mae-Li. She whispered something to Master Coles, something that sounded like "I'm sorry I'm late."

She came! Gabe thought. *She's here! She loves me!*

As Rosemary walked to the back of the studio she glanced at Gabe. He wasn't sure whether it was a smile or a frown.

Is she mad at me? Gabe wondered. *Why would she be mad at me? I only kissed her.*

Kissed her!

Gabe squeezed his eyes shut. Why did he have to do something so totally lame? What had he been thinking?

Will Rosemary ever speak to me again?

Gabe tried not to look at Rosemary as the class practiced karate. But with an entire wall covered with mirrors, it wasn't easy.

As Gabe circled David Betanahu, he caught a glimpse of Rosemary in the mirror. She was skillfully sparring with her new partner, Tim.

What could be more painful than watching the woman you love grapple with another man? Gabe wondered. *Nothing!*

That's when Gabe's new hero, Mike Chat, appeared in the classroom. No one else seemed to see him. But Gabe did.

Mike Chat stood behind Gabe and whispered into his ear, "The answer lies within you, Gabriel. And you alone. You must find your strength. Your focus. Your determination."

Gabe took in everything as he circled David. Then it happened. The power of Mike Chat began surging through his body!

"*Hee-yaaaa!*" Gabe shouted as he flipped David onto the mat over and over and over again!

Wham! Wham! Wham!

Poor David Betanahu, Gabe thought, as he worked him over. *He's just an innocent victim in all this. Collateral damage in this love affair.*

After fifteen minutes of abuse, David looked like shredded lettuce. But Gabe felt much better. He had finally found his strength and determination.

And he was determined to hold onto Rosemary!

Later, as the class sat in a circle, Gabe planted himself directly across from Rosemary. From there he watched her every move. The way her eye twitched. The way her mouth curled in a smile. He tried to read her face for any clues that would reveal how she really felt about him.

She loves me, Gabe thought. *She loves me not. Loves me. Not. Not.*

It was hopeless. By 3:51, Gabe had descended into total madness!

"Okay," Master Coles said. "Who wants to take their yellow belt exam?"

Gabe felt his hand shoot up in the air. "Me!" he heard himself shout.

All eyes turned to Gabe. He had a feeling he answered way too fast. But earning his yellow belt was the only way he could get close to Rosemary. He had to be in her league!

"Okay, Gabe," Master Coles said. "Let's do it."

Gabe joined Master Coles in the front of the studio. Then the two of them began to spar.

Come on, Mike Chat, Gabe thought as they circled. *Don't let me down.*

Gabe smiled as Mike Chat appeared in the classroom. The Master of Masters would coach him all the way.

"Let's see your *mai te zuki* now, Gabe," Master Coles said.

Mai te zuki, Gabe thought. *What do I do?*

"Drop and twist to the right," Mike Chat whispered to Gabe. "Left shoulder to the floor."

Gabe focused on his moves. Soon he was performing a perfect *mai te zuki*.

"Very nice," Master Coles said.

"Excellent, Gabriel!" Mike Chat exclaimed excitedly. "Excellent!"

Gabe sneaked a peak at Rosemary. She was nodding her head as if she approved. Tim Staples looked impressed, too. . . . The creep!

Mike Chat coached Gabe all through his moves. Finally, Master Coles picked up a board and held it up for Gabe to break. Gabe knew it was the last part of his yellow belt exam.

This is it, Gabe thought. *All that stands between me and Rosemary is a half-inch piece of plywood.*

"Be the board, Gabe," Mike Chat whispered into his ear. "Be the board."

Be the board, Gabe repeated in his mind.

Gabe focused on the wood in Master Coles's hands. He was centered. He was ready. He was the board.

"Yaaa!" Gabe shouted, as he thrust his hand at the plywood. But then—

"Eeeeeeyooooowwwwwww!!

Gabe saw stars as he dropped to his knees. His hand felt like it shattered into a million pieces!

"Ahhhhhh! Ahhhhhhh!" Gabe wailed, clutching his broken hand. "Ahhhhh!"

Through his howls he stared at the other kids. They were sitting on the floor staring back. Tim was doing a good job trying not to laugh. As for Rosemary, she looked horrified. Rosemary's face was the last thing Gabe remembered. Because right after that, he blacked out!

"Guess this is the end of karate, huh?" Adam asked.

Gabe looked up at his father. The two of them were sitting in the emergency room at Roosevelt Hospital. Gabe's right wrist had just been wrapped in a white fiberglass cast. He didn't know what hurt more—his hand or his pride.

"I'm a place kicker, Dad." Gabe sighed.

"Not just any place kicker," Adam said. "You're the future of place kicking. You've got a gift, Gabe."

"Whatever." Gabe sighed.

Leslie raced into the emergency room. Her jaw dropped when she saw the cast on Gabe's hand.

"I came as soon as I heard," Leslie said, running over to Gabe. "What happened?"

"Big guy tried a little too hard for his yellow belt, that's what," Adam said.

Gabe felt too ashamed to look at his mom. How could he let this happen? How could he make such a jerk of himself in front of the whole class? In front of Rosemary?

"How about a little ice cream on the way home?" Leslie asked with a small smile.

"No thanks," Gabe mumbled.

"You sure?" Leslie asked. "Not even Rocky Road?"

Gabe shook his head. Ice cream used to be the answer to all of his problems. But that was when life wasn't so complicated. Life before Rosemary.

"I'm sure," Gabe said. "Can we just get out of here already?"

The three of them left the hospital. As Gabe rode silently in the taxi between his mom and dad, he thought about Rosemary. Was it the end for him and her? Was two and a half weeks all the time they would ever have?

Maybe she'll call and ask about my hand, Gabe thought, *unless she doesn't care.*

Once home, Gabe took the phone into his bedroom. He sat on his bed and stared at it. He wanted to call Rosemary but he couldn't. That would be so weak.

From this moment on I will not be weak, Gabe proclaimed to himself. *I will not be—*

Rrrrrrinnnnng!

Gabe dove for the phone. He reached out with his broken hand to pick up the receiver, but quickly switched to the other.

"Hello?" Gabe said.

"Hello, Mrs. Burton?" Rosemary asked.

Gabe perked up at the sound of Rosemary's voice. He didn't even care that she thought he was his mom!

"No," Gabe said. "This is Gabe—"

"Hello?" a voice cut in.

Gabe groaned. What a time for his mom to pick up the other phone!

"I got it, Mom," Gabe said.

"Who is it?" Leslie asked.

"I got it!" Gabe repeated.

He waited until he heard a click. Then he quickly said hi.

"Hi," Rosemary said. "How's your hand?"

She does care, Gabe thought happily. *She really cares!*

He could see Rosemary in his mind. She was probably sitting cross-legged on her pink bedspread with her pink princess phone pressed to her ear.

"My hand? Fine. Barely hurts," Gabe lied.

"I just got so worried when you lost consciousness," Rosemary said.

Gabe gulped as he remembered that horrific

incident. He had wanted to block the whole thing out. But Rosemary's concern made him feel all warm and fuzzy inside. Like a genuine Hallmark moment!

"Yeah," Gabe said, "but it was just for a second. No big deal."

"What color cast did you get?" Rosemary asked.

"Just a plain one," Gabe replied.

"My cousin got this Incredible Hulk one," Rosemary said.

"Yeah, they had that," Gabe said. "I'm not that into the Hulk."

This is no time for small talk, Gabe thought. *It's time to lay things out on the table. To reach through the phone line and dig into her soul!*

"So . . . when can we hang out?" Gabe asked.

Silence.

"Um," Rosemary said. "You know, it's a really crazy weekend for me."

"It is?" Gabe asked.

It's Thursday night and she's going to camp Sunday morning, he thought. *Who cares how crazy the weekend is?*

"I've got the rehearsal dinner tomorrow night," Rosemary explained. "Wedding on Saturday. Camp Sunday."

Gabe chewed at his bottom lip.

Where's her whole "wish you could come to the wedding?" He wondered. *Where's that Rosemary? The Rosemary I loved. Not this alien with her crazy weekends!*

Gabe heaved a big sigh.

Okay, he thought. *Maybe I said a few things I shouldn't have.*

"Your new sparring partner coming to the wedding?" Gabe snapped.

"What?" Rosemary asked. "You mean Tim?"

"Is that what you call him?" Gabe demanded. "Are you calling him after you call me?"

Gabe couldn't believe it. The words were pouring out fast and furiously like a spigot. Like explosive vomit!

"What are you talking about?" Rosemary demanded.

"I'm talking about you and Tim Staples sitting in a tree!" Gabe started to shout. "First comes love, then comes marriage, then comes Tim Staples in a baby carriage!"

"You sound crazy, you know that?" Rosemary said.

"Why don't you have time this weekend?" Gabe asked. "Give me one good reason."

"I'm sorry, Gabe," Rosemary said. "But I haven't even packed for camp yet."

Who does she think she is? Gabe thought, gritting his teeth. *Kicking me to the curb like some loser?*

Gabe's anger grew red-hot. Until he finally shouted into the phone, "I hate you!"

More silence.

"What?" Rosemary gasped.

Her voice sounded more hurt than angry. But Gabe didn't care. He was hurting, too. And it was all because of Rosemary!

"I hate you! I hate you!" Gabe shouted even louder.

"Well, I hate you, too!" Rosemary shouted back.

"I hate you more!" Gabe yelled at the top of his lungs.

"How can you say something so mean?" Rosemary yelled back. "I hate you!"

Gabe winced as Rosemary slammed down her phone. He slammed down his phone, too. His broken wrist throbbed like crazy, but it was no match for the pain of his broken heart. As Gabe sat on his bed he could feel the hurt rising to the surface. But no way would he break down and cry. Not over her!

He struggled hard to fight back the tears, but then

his lip began to quiver. His shoulders began to shake. His mouth dropped open, and he began to wail.

"Ahhhhhh! Ahhhhhh! Ahhhhhh!"

Gabe was wracking with sobs when his dad rapped on his door.

"You okay in there, big guy?" Adam asked through the door.

Gabe froze. He couldn't let anyone know how a girl ruined him, not even his dad. He pulled himself together, gave one hard sniff, and said, "I'm cool, Dad."

Gabe waited until he heard Adam's feet move away from the door. Then he went back to being a blubbering mess.

How could this happen? Gabe wondered as he writhed around on his bed.

He had gotten hurt a million times—skinned knees, bloody nose, chipped tooth—even a broken wrist. But he had never known such pain before. A pain that made him cry an endless river of tears!

The door opened. Leslie quietly walked into the room. She sat down on the bed next to Gabe and put her arm around his shoulder.

"Maybe not everything is supposed to last forever, Gabe," Leslie said gently. "Certain things are like . . .

like skywriting. This really beautiful thing that lasts a couple moments, then it blows away."

Gabe stared up at his mom through a blur of tears.

Then he laid his head on her shoulder and began to sob.

Why did Rosemary Telesco ever have to walk into my life? Gabe wondered. *Why? Why? Why?*

When Gabe woke up the next morning his eyes were red and swollen. But he couldn't cry anymore. After a whole night of sobbing, Gabe was all cried out.

He planted himself in front of a rain-streaked window and stared out at West End Avenue. The weather reflected his mood—dark and stormy.

Gabe looked across the street into the other windows. Then he frowned. People were going about their lives—eating breakfast, reading the paper, gearing up to go outside in the rain.

Look at them, Gabe thought, his eyes narrowing. *Rats in their cages. Their lives destroyed by love!*

Gabe turned to look at his dad. Adam was struggling to fold up his sofa bed.

Look what love did to Dad, Gabe thought. *But that won't ever happen to me. I'm done with love. Done with it!*

Gabe sighed and turned back to the window.

I won't be like them, Gabe thought. *The fools!*

It rained buckets almost the whole day. When it finally slowed to a drizzle Gabe decided to go outside. His broken wrist kept him from shooting hoops, but that was okay with him. Gabe didn't feel like seeing Max, Sam, or Jacob—or anyone. He just wanted to be alone with his scooter and his despair.

As Gabe rolled his scooter into the elevator, he hardly looked at Ralph. He just stood there hanging his head.

"I remember my first girl," Ralph blurted.

Gabe rolled his eyes. Ralph always had a knack of reading people. Probably from riding hundreds of tenants up and down in the elevator hundreds of times a day.

"Met her at the Jersey shore," Ralph went on. "She was from Philly, I was from Brooklyn. So you know we were cursed from the start."

"Not right now, Ralph," Gabe mumbled, staring at the floor. "I'm really not in the mood."

The elevator came to a stop on the third floor.

Ralph's face brightened as he pulled the gate aside. Lina, the Swedish au pair, was pushing a toddler in a stroller into the elevator.

"*Hejsan,*" Ralph said. "*God morgon.*"

Gabe eyed Ralph with disgust. Now he was trying to impress Lina by speaking Swedish!

The dumb things guys do for women, Gabe thought. *Give me a break!*

Once outside, Gabe weaved his scooter around the puddles. He didn't know why he was riding toward Rosemary's block. Wasn't he in enough pain? What was he trying to do—torture himself?

But there he was, on 81st Street and Central Park West, standing a safe distance from Rosemary's building. He didn't know how long he stood gazing at her front door. But just as he was about to turn his scooter around, he saw her!

Rosemary was walking out of the building with her parents. The whole family was dressed up as if they were going out to dinner.

Dinner! Gabe remembered. *The wedding rehearsal dinner is tonight.*

The doorman hailed a taxi. He held the door as the Telescos stepped inside.

There she goes, Gabe thought.

But as the doorman shut the door, something strange happened.

Gabe didn't care how pretty Rosemary looked in her flowered skirt and sleeveless top. He didn't care if Rosemary was thinking about Tim Staples instead of him. In fact, for the first time since that horrible day yesterday, Gabe didn't care about Rosemary Telesco at all!

He watched as the taxi pulled away. Then he turned his scooter and kicked it all the way home.

Saturday morning Gabe woke to a room bathed in sunlight. He climbed out of bed and walked to the window. Pulling up the Venetian blinds he smiled. The rain had stopped. The sun was shining. The storm was over in more ways than one. Gabe had recovered from his bout of lovesickness and he was ready to face the world!

I'm going to be okay! Gabe thought.

After a good breakfast Gabe and his dad did what they always did on Saturday mornings. They headed to Riverside Park for some serious place kicking.

I don't need Rosemary, Gabe thought, as he booted one ball after another. *You come into the world alone and you leave alone. So who needs anyone?*

Gabe's next kick sent the football sailing over the trees. His dad whistled as it disappeared into the horizon. Gabe knew it was one of his best kicks ever. So why didn't he give a hoot?

Uh-oh, Gabe thought. *I guess I'm not really okay.*

Adam rested his hand on Gabe's shoulder. "How about some ice cream, G-Man?" he asked.

"Okay, Dad." Gabe sighed.

The two left Riverside Park and headed for Gabe's favorite ice cream shop on Broadway. After buying cones, they sat side by side on a bench outside. Gabe held the cone with his good hand while resting his cast on his lap.

"Dad?" Gabe asked between licks.

"Yeah, Gabe?" Adam asked.

"What's the deal with girls?" Gabe asked. "I mean, why are they the way they are?"

Adam heaved a big sigh. Then he said, "You're talking to the wrong man, Gabe."

Gabe didn't care that his dad was a loser at love. He needed answers—and he needed them now!

"How come all love has to come to an end?" Gabe asked.

Adam quietly licked his mint chocolate chip cone.

Then he turned to Gabe and said, "Let me tell you something about me and your mom. Once upon a time we really loved each other. But over time there just got to be all these things we left unsaid. And all those things started to pile up like the clutter in our storage locker."

Gabe watched his dad so closely that his ice cream dripped down his hand. Adam looked so sad talking about his marriage. But he kept on talking as if he had to get it off his chest. . . .

"After a while," Adam went on, "there were so many little things we didn't say to each other that we hardly said anything to each other anymore."

"Why don't you just say them, Dad?" Gabe asked.

Adam shrugged. "I don't know, Gabe," he said. "I kind of wish I had."

Gabe and Adam sat in silence finishing their cones. *Who was I kidding?* Gabe wondered. *I'm not going to get any comfort here. What Dad knows about love can fill a small pamphlet!*

Adam popped the last piece of his cone into his mouth. He stood up, brushed off his hands, and said, "Let's knock over a hot dog stand on the way home."

Gabe stared off into the distance. He loved hot

dogs almost as much as ice cream. But he shook his head and said, "I think I'm going to just hang out a little bit."

"Clear your head?" Adam asked.

"Yeah," Gabe said. "Clear my head."

"You got it, champ," Adam said. He picked up the bag of footballs and slung them over his shoulder. "You kicked good today. You're at least the Big Ten."

"Thanks," Gabe said. "It felt good."

Gabe licked the last of his cone as he watched his dad cross Broadway.

It's not fair, Gabe thought. *I thought I was over Rosemary. For good. Why does she keeping popping back into my head like this?*

Somewhere a million miles away the girl he once loved was walking down an aisle in a blue dress, daintily tossing rose petals onto the carpet.

She's going down her road, Gabe thought, *and I'm stuck back on mine.*

Gabe finished his ice cream and stood up. Then he began walking aimlessly through the streets of New York. As he passed the Beacon Theater he saw words flashing across the marquee. They read, "I Love You, Rosemary!"

Gabe squeezed his eyes shut. When he opened

them again, the words read, "Elvis Costello. One Night Only."

I'm losing it, Gabe thought. *I'm really losing it.*

He walked down Broadway thinking about what his dad had said. There were things he never said to Rosemary, too. And lots of things he never should have said!

A bus rolled by. The colorful ad on the side read, "I'm Sorry, Rosemary!"

Picking up speed, he walked past a wall covered with graffiti. Instead of tags the words declared, "I don't hate you! I could never hate you!"

Gabe stopped to stare at the wall. Part of it was plastered with movie posters that read, "Don't Go to Camp! Kiss Me Again!"

Gabe couldn't believe it. There, right before his eyes, were all the things he should have said to Rosemary. But it was too late.

I've got to get away from all this! Gabe thought in a panic. *I've got to get away!*

He began walking downtown, faster and faster. But there was no escape from all the things he never said to Rosemary!

Gabe squeezed through the crowd in front of the 68th Street movie theater. Scrolling across the marquee were the words, "I love you! I love you! I love you!"

Gabe stared at the marquee. Suddenly he knew what he had to do. He turned up 68th Street and began running toward the park as fast as he could!

Love isn't about ridiculous little words, Gabe decided as he raced through Central Park. It's about airplanes pulling banners over stadiums. It's about marriage proposals on Jumbotrons. It's about sappy soap operas!

And in Gabe's case, it was about getting Loston Harris to sing at Rosemary's aunt's wedding!

14

Gabe sprinted out of the park.

He ran one block over to Madison Avenue and the Carlyle Hotel. The same hotel where Gabe and Rosemary had shared a loveseat and listened to Loston Harris. The same hotel where Gabe had held Rosemary's hand for the first time!

Gabe caught his breath. Then he dodged through the front door of the fancy hotel.

"Mr. Harris!" Gabe called as he entered the dark lounge. "Loston Harris!"

Gabe looked around. The tables were empty. Only a waiter stood in the room placing glass candleholders on the tables. The dark-haired man looked up at Gabe and smiled. "Sorry, my friend," he said with a Latin accent. "Mr. Harris is gone. He's playing the

Montreal Jazz Festival."

Gone? Gabe's heart started to pound. He can't be! Not today!

"But I need him to help me get my girlfriend back!" Gabe said in a single breath. "He has to sing at her aunt's wedding."

"You have a girlfriend?" the waiter asked.

"I did," Gabe said. "Her name is Rosemary."

"Is Rosemary your first girlfriend, amigo?" the waiter asked.

Gabe nodded and said, "My first and only."

A dreamy smile spread across the waiter's face. "I remember my first," he said. "Her name was Isabella Catone. My sister's friend. I can still smell her hair, today."

"I can still smell Rosemary's hair too," Gabe said with a smile. "It smells like strawberry."

Gabe couldn't believe it.

He and this twenty-something guy were talking about their old girlfriends—as if they had been best buds all their lives!

"Isabella was my first," the waiter went on, "but she wasn't my only."

Gabe wrinkled his brow. "What are you saying?" he asked.

"You may not know this now," the waiter said gently. "But there will be others. So, so many others."

"But I don't want others," Gabe argued. "One was bad enough!"

The waiter nodded as if he understood. "Women are a curse on us, amigo," he sighed. "A wonderful, remarkable, horrible curse."

Gabe stared at the waiter with the Spanish accent. This guy seemed to have more perspective than Confucius.

"You don't happen to sing, do you?" Gabe asked.

The waiter laughed as he went back to his candles. Gabe left the hotel, still thinking about those simple words of truth—how there would be other girls in his life. So, so many other girls . . .

"Yeah, right!" Gabe muttered.

I never heard anything so dumb in my life! Gabe decided. *There's only one girl on this planet for me. It's Rosemary Telesco—or no one!*

Gabe knew the next thing he had to do. He raced over to Fifth Avenue and then back into Central Park.

"Rosemary!" Gabe gasped, out of breath.

He darted past Umpire Rock, sprinted past Hecksher Playground, weaved around sunbathers on Sheep Meadow and bike riders on the mall. When he reached the bluff overlooking the lake, he gazed down.

There it is! Gabe thought, trying to catch his breath. *The Boathouse.*

Gabe's heart pounded as he ran down the rocks. It beat even faster as he walked into the Boathouse.

Where is she? Gabe wondered as he looked around. *Where's Rosemary?*

The band broke into some jazzy number. Gabe's eyes swept across the dance floor. He saw lots of twirling, gyrating people, but not Rosemary. He was about to turn toward the buffet table when his eye caught a flash of blue. It was Rosemary wearing her blue dress and sitting at the side of the dance floor. She looked bored but beautiful as she eyed the dancers. A ring of flowers around her hair was beginning to wilt.

Gabe watched as Rosemary leaned back in her chair. Suddenly her eyes locked with his.

She sees me! Gabe thought in a panic. *What will she do next? Ignore me? Call me a jerk? Make a scene and kick me out?*

Rosemary stood up. Then she walked across the dance floor toward Gabe.

"What are you doing here?" Rosemary asked. Her voice sounded more confused than angry.

"You're going to camp tomorrow," Gabe said. "I . . . I wanted to say good-bye."

"I thought you hate me," Rosemary said.

"I don't," Gabe said. "I lied."

Gabe was proud of his honesty. He wasn't going to be like his father. He wasn't going to let all the things left unsaid smother him.

But there was still one thing left to be said. The most important thing of all . . .

"I love you, Rosemary!" Gabe declared.

"You . . . what?" Rosemary asked.

"I do!" Gabe threw back his shoulders and let the words gush out. "I love you more than anyone has ever loved. I'm sorry. But I love you. I love you. I love you!

There. I did it, Gabe thought. *I let it all hang out there!*

But as Rosemary stood in total silence it kept on hanging. And hanging. And hanging. And hanging.

"Um," Gabe finally said. "Do you think . . . um . . . you might love me, too?"

"I don't know what I think," Rosemary said.

Gabe's mouth dropped open. After he poured his heart out to Rosemary, this was her answer? She didn't know?

"What?" Gabe asked.

"I'm only eleven," Rosemary said with a shrug. "I don't think I'm ready to be in love."

Gabe was thunderstruck. He expected Rosemary to jump into his arms and tell him she loved him, too. Just like in the movies!

"I'm not ready either," Gabe said, waving his arms. "But I'm doing it!"

"Then maybe I was wrong," Rosemary said.

"Wrong about what?" Gabe asked.

"Maybe girls don't mature faster," Rosemary said.

"They do!" Gabe said. "You know they do. You said it at the park. We at least mature at the same rate."

The flowers around Rosemary's head bounced as she shook her head. "I don't know what mature is anymore," she said with a sigh.

As Gabe looked at Rosemary he didn't know what to say. What else could he say? They were just two kids after all.

The band began playing "Last Dance." Almost everyone at the wedding jammed on the dance floor in front of the band.

"Um," Rosemary said. "Do you want to . . . dance?"

"Dance?" Gabe repeated. "Um, sure. Why not?"

Gabe and Rosemary joined the others on the dance floor. They rested their heads on each other's shoulders. Then they swayed slowly to the music.

Careful not to re-crush his broken hand, Gabe held on to Rosemary for dear life. He knew the truth and he was pretty sure Rosemary did, too. Tomorrow she would be off to camp and eventually to private school.

Gabe took a whiff of Rosemary's strawberry-scented hair. It was the last dance of the wedding—and for them.

When the song was over Gabe said good-bye to Rosemary. Then he dragged himself out of the Boathouse and all the way home.

"Hey, Mr. Gabe!" Ralph said as he slid the elevator gate. "How goes it?"

Gabe stepped into the elevator and smiled.

"Hey, Ralph," he said. "I'm—"

"Hold the door please!" a voice cut in.

Gabe turned to see Lina, the Swedish au pair, running toward the elevator. But this time she wasn't alone or with a toddler in a stroller. She was with a guy!

Lina and the guy squeezed into the elevator and

exchanged a kiss. Gabe glanced over at Ralph as he slid the gate shut with a loud bang.

Hey, pal, I know the feeling, Gabe thought. *But you come into the world alone and you leave it the exact same way. Love ends. And that's just the way things are.*

Gabe used his keys to open the door to his apartment. The first thing he noticed when he walked inside was the silence.

"Hello?" Gabe called.

No answer.

Gabe walked into the kitchen and opened the fridge. As he pulled out a plastic container of orange juice he checked out the side. Did it belong to his mom or his dad?

Gabe turned it all the way around in his hand. There was no label. And no name.

Hmm, Gabe thought. *You don't see that every day.*

He was about to grab a glass when he heard voices. There was laughter coming from the other room—his mom's room!

He put down the orange juice, left the kitchen, and walked over to his mom's door. Opening it just a crack he peeked inside.

A sixteen-year-old girl and a nineteen-year-old boy were sitting at the foot of the bed laughing together.

Gabe recognized them. They were his parents when they were young, the same ages they were when they met at camp!

Gabe blinked hard. When his eyes opened he saw his real parents. They were twenty-three years older and they were still laughing!

What was up with that?

"Mom? Dad?" Gabe asked. "Is everything . . . okay?"

Leslie turned and smiled at Gabe. "Oh, sure!" she said. "We were just remembering how horrible our honeymoon went."

Adam cracked up as he fell back on the bed.

"Key West!" Leslie went on. "Everything that could possibly go wrong did."

"Unlimited disaster," Adam guffawed. "Tropical storm, lost luggage, . . ."

Gabe couldn't stop staring at his mom and dad. Were his eyes tricking him? Or were his parents laughing it up together and having a good time?

"Are you hungry, Gabe?" Leslie asked. "Should we go out for dinner?"

"You mean . . . all of us?" Gabe asked.

Adam nodded. "We can run down to the place on the corner," he said. "Like we used to."

Gabe smiled from ear to ear. The last time they all went out for dinner together, he was practically in a booster seat. He still didn't get it, but he was beginning to like it!

"Sure," Gabe said. "The place at the corner sounds good."

Leslie and Adam jumped off the bed.

"Now I want us all to wear jackets," Leslie said. "It may be summer but the nights are still pretty cool."

Gabe watched his mom leave the room. He looked over at his dad for some kind of explanation.

"I cleared out some things from the storage locker," Adam whispered.

"Oh!" Gabe whispered back.

Fifteen minutes later Gabe and his parents were sitting in their favorite booth in the corner diner. They were eating together, talking together, and laughing together. Just like one big happy family.

As the waiter placed their dishes on the table, Gabe gazed out the window. People were strolling up and down the streets. Some were alone. Some were walking dogs. Some were walking hand in hand with partners.

Love is an ugly, terrible business practiced by fools, Gabe decided. *It will trample your heart and leave you bleeding on the floor. And where does it get you in the end? Just a couple of lousy memories you can't ever shake—no matter how hard you try!*

As Gabe dumped ketchup on his fries, memories of Rosemary drifted through his head: He and Rosemary in karate class. He and Rosemary riding the subway together. He and Rosemary kissing awkwardly under the awning of her apartment building. He and Rosemary riding his scooter up the Hudson River bike path.

Gabe smiled slowly to himself.

Love ends.

But sometimes it's worth it!